# Log Cabin Miracles

## DATE DUE

©2013

No part                                        a retrieval

system                                        e written

permis

ISBN 1

ISBN 1

Printed

Bible V                                        slation

# Dedication

This book is dedicated to my five grandchildren,
Ryan, Carrie, Mark, Matthew, and Michael.

# Chapter 1

Ryan Downing stood on the screened-in porch of the rustic mountain cabin. Unhurriedly, he sipped the steaming hot coffee. The emanating white swirls from the coffee mug spiraled upwards and arched into the early morning coolness. He could hear the extra-thick bacon popping and sizzling in the kitchen. It was a fresh spring morning that was transitioning early into the mountain summer. The sun in the east was stealthily emerging from the shady mountain background, slowly climbing upwards towards the tops of the tall lofty evergreens and pine trees. Splendored with pink, orange, and blue sky, it was a scintillatingly magnificent morning day in June of 2009.

Ryan was a Christian book author. He had been writing since about 4:00 AM. Early mornings were his most prolific writing times of day. "Early to rise... early to start..." He sat down on the plump soft cushion in one of the two antique rocking chairs.

Nancy, Ryan's girlfriend, had purchased the rocking chairs. She was always traveling around and browsing garage sales. She had paid extra for the garage sale owner's son, to deliver the rocking chairs in his pick-up truck. She accompanied the delivery and rode up in the truck, with the confirmation that he would escort her back into town, about an hour away. Nancy, had indeed, decorated most of his cabin. Ryan was happy to reimburse her for all the "bargains." She was always finding some garage sale antique-looking item that just seemed to fit both the cabin's décor and his personality. Nancy, like Ryan, was also a writer. She frequently was a speaker at various women's Bible Study gatherings. Ryan was an author-speaker who regularly gave presentations all across the United States at Men's Bible Study meetings, a variety of churches, book signings, and at Bluegrass Gospel Jam festivals. He was nationally known as the "Bluegrass Gospel Jam Ambassador." Earlier this year, he had completed his latest book, "Bluegrass Gospel Jams."

Ryan went inside to the kitchen. He flipped over the sizzling bacon strips. He grabbed a yellow Pyrex bowl from below the kitchen counter, opened the refrigerator, and picked out three "grade-A" large eggs from the carton. He brought out the half-full gallon plastic jug of one percent milk. He also took out the cream cheese container and placed it on the counter beside the Thomas' bagels bag. He whipped up the eggs and milk mixture with a wire whip. After the bacon strips started sizzling more slowly, he placed the browning thick bacon strips on a paper towel to drain and become crisp. With a large spatula-like spoon, he removed most of the excess grease. He poured the scrambled egg mixture into the skillet and added salt and pepper. Immediately the eggs started congealing and forming a brownish yellow color. The distinctive bacon aroma still permeated the whole cabin. He added some

"Pace" mild salsa. As a garnish on the breakfast plate, he chopped up a golden yellow banana and sliced up some fresh deep red ripe strawberries. He took his breakfast feast outside to the porch. The rising morning sun quickly and steadily inundated the porch. He positioned his "Elk" plate on the Ethan Allen antique table between the two garage-sale rocking chairs. He went back into the kitchen and brought out the blue and white-spotted insulated ceramic coffee pot. He refilled hot coffee into his mug, reheating the cooling bottom half of his "rainbow trout" coffee mug.

Mornings were his favorite time of day. If he were in town, he would already be at a restaurant, sipping coffee, reading his Bible, reading a chapter in one of his own books, and having a "Senior Sunriser" breakfast. He also enjoyed an "Eggs Petite" breakfast at another restaurant. Recently, he found another breakfast delight, a "Senior Burrito" garnished with Cholula hot sauce. Going out to breakfast was a special treat for Ryan. Despite all his troubles, double by-pass heart surgery, and hardships over the comeback years, he always managed to have breakfast out at a restaurant. Now that he was here at the cabin for most of the summer, he didn't mind fixing a breakfast meal for himself every once in a while. Breakfast was his favorite feast...

"... starting the day off right."

Summer time was a recharge retreat. His original four books were all on the subject of "The Pursuit of Peace." He continually challenged himself to adhere and abide by his own peace principles. As he stated in his books, it was always easy to get "too busy." But up here in the mountain setting, it was easy "to back up and stay on track." Earlier this morning, he had already completed his Bible reading. He had also read the chapter, "This Is It!" in his second published book, "Pursuit of Peace Doubts, Prayers, and Victories." He was just beginning to initiate an email campaign to help market his new book. Ryan had learned to self-publish. He had also learned how to put up a "Bluegrass Gospel Jam" website and blog on the Internet.

After consuming his breakfast delicacies, he sipped the still-steaming coffee as the aroma spiraled into the morning freshness. He listened to the squirrel chatter, the tufting wind gusts, and the swishing aspen trees. He went inside and washed off his dishes with hot water and a scrubbing sponge. He resisted the temptation to leave the dirty dishes in the sink. If he washed dishes as he went, it was always easier to keep the kitchen clean. He returned the milk carton, salsa, and bagels to their appropriate places. Now the kitchen was sparkling and welcoming for any guests who might stop by. Ryan didn't have guests that often, but he enjoyed having things in order, and fresh. Today was different. This afternoon, a new guest was arriving.

He poured a small glass of "pulp orange juice." He drank all of it in one long drink and rinsed the glass. Ryan picked up the unfolded letter. He took the letter out to the porch, sat down, and refilled his trout mug. His fingers encircled the mug, absorbing the warmness. The yawning wind softly meandered through the tops of the trees, as if the sun were telling the wind and forest to wake up and get busy. A bright warm spring day was arriving. The mountains and natural nature were communicating with his thoughts.

He began re-reading the five-page folded letter. The last page was a photocopy of a legal order official letter from the judge of the court. He began recalling the two conversations that had transpired over the recent past few weeks...

"Hi Ryan, Quentin Paisley here." Quentin's gravely voice over the phone sounded a little more weak than usual, but still authoritative. "How about having breakfast with me this Friday, at Perkins?" Quentin's voice seemed a little slurred.

"Yes, I would enjoy that," replied Ryan. "What time?"

"How about 8:30?"

"OK. I will see you there, at 8:30."

"All right..." Quentin's voice trailed off.

He jotted down the appointment in his Day-Timer. Eight thirty was a late breakfast for Ryan. He was usually having breakfast between 6:00 and 6:30, but he knew Quentin was arising later and later. "That would be OK," he thought, "I can use the time to do more writing before I meet with him." The Perkins restaurant was an hour's traveling distance from Ryan's cabin. He always enjoyed the trip, down and back, following the winding mountain highway through Poudre River Canyon.

He first met Quentin at one of the very first Bluegrass Gospel Jams. That particular Saturday evening, a little while after the Bluegrass Gospel Jam had already started, Quentin came shuffling in with assistance from a curly knotty-wood cane. He sat on the last end seat of the folding chairs on the back row. Quentin had snowy white ashen hair. Both gnarled hands gripped his walking stick. Ryan observed Quentin's "half-curl-smile" indicating that he seemed to really enjoy the lively fast-paced bluegrass gospel songs. The gospel songs were old church hymns, sung in fast-picking bluegrass style. At the end of the Jam, Ryan began making a few last-minute announcements, inviting everyone to come back in two weeks for another "Good Old Bluegrass Gospel Jam."

"... and by the way, I have some booklets I wrote on "The Pursuit of Peace." They are free. I only ask that you pass them on to someone else after you read them. There is a bowl on the back counter if you would like to make a donation to help cover the costs and expansion of the Jams. For our final song, we will do, 'Will the Circle be Unbroken.'" During the finale song, Quentin got up and shuffled out towards the back. Ryan was involved in having different musicians do instrumental breaks right after each chorus. They finished up the last song by doing an "Amen ending," with no instruments, just harmonizing voices, "In the sky, Lord...in the sky ......"

After loading the sound equipment into his Jeep, he went back to the counter where his booklets were displayed. A few of the booklets had disappeared. In the donation bowl were one five-dollar bill, some one-dollar bills, and some quarters and dimes. There was a check overturned in the bowl. He looked at the check. He was stunned. The check was for $100.00. Tears came to Ryan's eyes. "It must have been that old guy I didn't get to meet."

On Monday, Ryan retrieved Quentin's phone number from his check. He called Quentin and set up a breakfast appointment at Perkins restaurant. Quentin immediately told him that, "I was just getting ready to call you, Ryan." They agreed to meet at 7:30 A.M. on that next Friday. From that point on, he and Quentin started getting together at the same time every other Friday. They became good friends. Quentin didn't always attend all the Jams, but the every other week breakfast meetings became a regular routine. Even though there was a huge age difference, Ryan and Quentin became mutual encouragers and good friends. At the very first breakfast meeting, Quentin gave Ryan the keys, and permission, to use Quentin's cabin.

"I like the way you write, Ryan. It's like you are having a personal conversation with me. You don't force religion onto me; you just lay out practical examples that I can get a hold of in my mind. I want you to use the cabin to do more writing. You can invite guests to have a peace retreat, like you mentioned in your books, as long as you are physically there with your guests. I don't want the cabin rented out to just anybody, just people you know personally. It's in my will that I'm going to leave the cabin after I die to my grandson, Derek. But for now, I want you to use the cabin."

Ryan recalled that it had been over five years since that conversation had transpired. On the spot, Ryan accepted Quentin's offer. Ryan began using the cabin regularly all during the summer months, usually for two weeks at a time. These were very inspiring and proficient writing times for Ryan. He usually accomplished more writing in one summer than he accomplished all during the rest of the year. In-between the creative composing times, "fishing..." refueled his thinking mind. He had now written six books and was now working on his seventh book. During the other nine months of the year, He spent a lot of time traveling all across the United States speaking and setting up new Bluegrass Gospel Jams.

Now, five years later, over this past year, Quentin's health had begun rapidly deteriorating. The every-other-week Friday morning breakfast meetings still continued steadily and regularly. Quentin changed the time from 7:30 to 8:30 AM. Sometimes they didn't get together because of Ryan's speaking engagements. Quentin was now 85 years old. Ryan was 73 years old... "Two old friends mentoring and encouraging each other. The old guy and the young guy."

Last Friday, he met with Quentin again. Quentin did not show up until about 8:55. It was very unusual for Quentin to be late for an appointment. Like Ryan, Quentin almost always showed up early. As he sat down in the booth across from Ryan, Quentin did not look well. His wrinkled face was stretched downwards. He looked very frail, as if he had suddenly lost a lot of weight. He still had a smile. His twinkling azure eyes still had sparkle. Quentin was using an aluminum walker now. He had also started carrying an oxygen bottle with him, with a tube running up to his nose. Surprisingly strong, he grabbed and fervently shook Ryan's hand.

"Thanks for coming, Ryan. Sorry I was late."

"I wouldn't think of missing our breakfast appointment time," Ryan replied.

The two friends ordered their regular "standing order" individual breakfasts. However, Quentin only ate about one-fourth of his breakfast. He pushed the plate back and said, "That new medicine the doctor put me on has caused me to lose my whole appetite. The food always looks good, but then I just don't feel like eating it. How is your new book coming, Ryan? Have you decided on a title yet?"

"You know me, Quentin. I never tell anyone about my books until I finish, even the title. However, today, I do have my most recent finished book with me, 'Bluegrass Gospel Jams.' I brought you a personally autographed copy.

The waitress came by, refilled Ryan's coffee cup, and picked up both plates, both his, and Quentin's three-fourths still-full plate. Quentin sipped on his "Sleepy Time" hot tea. Ryan thanked the waitress for refilling his coffee. Quentin's gravely voice was very low and guttural. Ryan leaned forward so he could hear.

"Thanks for the book. I always look forward to reading your books." Quentin paused. "I have a proposition for you, Ryan. Before I make this proposition to you, I have some background information you need to know."

"OK." Ryan never really knew what to expect from this old-man friend. Quentin always came up with new insights on different situations.

"Do you remember what I told you about the cabin when I first gave you permission to use the cabin?"

"Boy, do I? When you first made that offer, I about fell off my chair," replied Ryan. "You said that you had it in your will that your grandson, Derek, would inherit the cabin upon your death. I was always curious why you didn't plan on passing it on to your son, Jasper Paisley. Why didn't you plan on passing it on to your son?"

"That's a good question that I really don't have a good answer for. While I was working and being self-employed, my son, Jasper, and I never got along. We have never been close, even now. He said I never spent enough time with him while he was growing up, that I never ever considered anything about his feelings. The truth is that Jasper was always angry at something. Jasper has spent his entire life worrying about everything. He never listened to me, or anyone else, really. He was selfish, and the chip on his shoulder seemed to interfere with every step of progress all along the way. I don't know why he became so cynical and overbearing. He was always mad at the world. He always griped and complained. Jasper's son, Derek, my grandson, became the opposite type personality. Derek didn't want to grow up and be like his dad. Derek left the house as soon as he could. Derek eventually became a produce manager at a large grocery store chain. Over the years, Derek and I got together up at the cabin. Those 'Derek visits' were enjoyable for me."

"Did Derek come up and go fishing?" asked Ryan.

"Yes. Derek came up, alone, several times, four or five times, I think, from Florida, on his vacation, usually for three days, one time for a week. We mostly just talked before and during meal times and over coffee afterwards by the fireplace. He enjoyed doing all the cooking. My body parts didn't allow me to go fishing with him. Those vacation times were quality conversation times. That's when I decided to give my cabin to Derek. I told him how important it was to slow down and refocus on the important things in life. I even gave him some of your books to read, Ryan, to help him set good priorities. He seemed to understand. Derek was an entirely different persona than his dad was." Quentin coughed and cleared his throat. Quentin's deep reverberating voice became concise.

In his mind, Ryan quickly pondered what was going to be said next. "Was he going to now lose the use of the cabin to Derek? What was Quentin leading up to? Was the cabin relationship now coming to an abrupt halt?"

Quentin stretched back, put both hands on the table, rubbed his straggly white pallid hair with both hands, adjusted the oxygen tube to his nose, wiped his running nose with a napkin, and stated in his solemnly deep resounding voice, "Ryan, I am giving you the cabin, now. It's my gift to you. My lawyer is preparing the warranty deed to be recorded Tuesday at the courthouse. Here is a copy of the deed." Quentin took out a piece of paper from his shirt pocket. The paper was folded into fourths.

"Is your legal name spelled correctly, Ryan?"

Ryan looked at the unfolded slightly wrinkled General Warranty Deed. The deed was dated for next Tuesday. The documentary fee was "0," indicating that the property would be deeded with no cash transferred.

"Yes," replied Ryan. "But why are you giving the cabin to me? I don't understand... I thought you were going to give it to your grandson, Derek. That's what I understood from the first day on, when you first offered to me the use

14

of your cabin, and I truly have made good use of the cabin. I appreciate what you are doing but I understand if you want to give the cabin to your grandson. What has changed your mind? And why are you attempting to give a piece of real estate for free... to me? This is really an enormous gift, Quentin."

"Well... I have seen, first hand, the results of how your 'Peace Books' books have helped people... including me. That's the primary reason. Also, as you might have observed, my health is rapidly losing ground. I only have a few weeks or months remaining to be here on this earth. I'm on hospice care right now and that's the beginning of the end. About seven months ago, my heart doctor enlightened me of what would be happening, and everything he said... is coming to pass ...almost right on schedule. So I won't be around much longer." Quentin stretched backward again, with both hands on the booth table. Like his firm handshake, in his authoritative solemnly serious voice, he leaned forward and continued his dissertation.

"My grandson, Derek, married a dental assistant he met in the dentist chair. Her name was Susanna. Susanna came from a very 'well-to-do' family. She was an only child, was spoiled, and had received her own way from day one. She grew up differently than most folks, without too much effort, and not having to work hard at much of anything. This is information I gleaned from conversations with Derek...

She did, however, have one ambition... to become a female dentist with a practice of her own. However, her hot temper and all-control-type personality seemed to always interfere with her progress. Her attitude was a lot like Derek's dad. She was a very pretty girl, but she enjoyed being antagonistic and confrontational, even with Derek, especially right after they were married. Derek was the calm, hard working, dedicated grocery store employee who never created problems for anyone. Susanna is still a dental assistant. She never made it to becoming a full-fledged dentist."

Quentin continued, "After that doomsday talk with my heart doctor, I decided to change my will ...regarding lots... of things. I decided to give the cabin to Derek right away, while I was still alive, before the distant 'hardly-ever-seen' relatives started fighting over my money and possessions. I called and talked to Derek and told him what my plans were. Derek said he would talk it over with Susanna. He said Susanna always, 'never wanted anything to do with a cabin in the mountains.'"

Derek said to me, "I could never talk Susanna into going on a vacation with me to Colorado. She always said she had 'professional designations' to work on."

"When Derek and Susanna had their baby, my great grandson, Porter, Derek said their married life went into an even more tumultuous turmoil. Susanna figured that the new visitor in her household 'took too much time,' and was a 'drag on her career.' She enjoyed having a baby... for the first few years. But then, she returned to working as a dental assistant. She always put in extra working hours. She also filled in extra hours during the week and sometimes on Saturdays for emergencies. She found babysitters who took care of Porter from 7:15 in the morning to 6:00 in the evening. She seldom cooked a meal, and usually brought home fast food and served it on 'curly-designed heavy Dixie plastic and paper plates.' Derek told me that evening family growing-up times were spent watching non-descript half-hour television programs. Susanna never encouraged or helped with Porter's school homework. She just continually ordered him to, 'Go and do it! You have to make your own way in this world, and you might as well learn it now!' Derek always seemed to have to work the late shift while Porter was in school. Going to school events, as a family function, never happened. Meal times were never regular."

Quentin continued, "This is more information Derek told me... Derek had given up his Produce Manager position to go over and work on the grocery side to learn to become a store manager. He wanted to get a promotion to make more money for his family. But the manager of the store had become a stumbling block to Derek's progress. Intrinsically, Derek knew that the manager's personality was contrary to Derek's. The meddlesome manager was always in active confrontation... with all the employees, and even store customers. However, Derek's desire to get ahead, and get promoted, overtook his thinking. Every week, Derek's workday schedule changed. Derek began working all the late shifts. He had a job of Assistant Manager 'responsibility,' which really meant that the Assistant Manager was responsible to close up the store at night. In addition, even though promises had been made, Derek's hours and pay were cut. He was earning less than he earned on the Produce Manager's daytime work schedule. As a result, Derek had very little after-school contact with Porter. Susanna let Porter exist pretty much all by himself. Gradually, Porter began becoming belligerent, selfish, and hard to deal with. Temper tantrums turned out to be more and more frequent. As Porter started getting older, the house grew noisy and loud. Derek said, 'The television became like a blaring air raid siren.' Not very much peace, there ..."

"Sounds like a not-so-good life for your great grandson," offered Ryan. "How did you find out about all this family information, with you living in Colorado and Derek living in Florida?"

"Oh, Derek and I talk a lot over the phone. I've tried to stay in touch with him as a 'great grandpa.' So I made deliberate phone calls on purpose. Derek is the only one in my family who I cared to talk to. But he never really opened up to me until these past few months. Earlier, our conversations were a little superficial. I didn't know about how his family life had soured...until these recent conversations happened these past few weeks..."

"A couple of months ago," continued Quentin, "Derek managed to talk Susanna into coming up to see the cabin on a short vacation. They flew up to Denver, rented a car, and drove up to the cabin. Porter stayed with a friend back in Florida. I met Derek and Susanna for a late breakfast before they headed up to the cabin. The mountains had just received about an inch of fresh snow."

"Susanna was cold," Derek said. "When they got to the cabin, Susanna was 'appalled' at the 'anti-urban' rustic cabin. Susanna did not want to spend the night there and even refused to stay the rest of the afternoon... She demanded that they go immediately back to town to a modern motel. Derek discussed with Susanna about Quentin's desire to give the cabin to them."

"We'll see about that!" she said.

"So they returned back to 'warm' Florida as soon as they could get the airline tickets changed. They didn't even get together with me before they left." Quentin paused, poised in deep thought.

"Shortly afterwards, I received a letter from Derek. I could tell that Susanna had forced Derek to write it. In the letter, they said they would accept the cabin only if I first made some improvements before they took the property. Susanna wanted me to install new carpeting and have the kitchen and bathroom remodeled, at my expense, before they would take the cabin."

Ryan interjected, "You mean they wanted you to put extra money in... before you gave them a free cabin, a piece of real estate that has value just sitting there?"

"I couldn't believe it either!" replied Quentin.

"That's really looking a gift horse in the mouth."

"Bottom line, Ryan, the cabin is now yours!"

The second conversation happened two weeks later. He and Quentin got together again at their normal breakfast location. This time the appointment was set for 9:00 AM.

"Ryan," began Quentin, "I have a special request for you. In fact... it's not probably very fair that I ask this of you..." The waitress came and took their order. Ryan sipped his coffee. Quentin sipped his Sleepy Time tea.

Quentin pulled out an envelope. "I have here, a letter from Derek. It's an apology letter for the way Susanna acted about the cabin gift...not from Susanna, but from Derek. I have a copy of it for you to take home with you today."

"I think Derek and Susanna are about to get divorced," Quentin continued. "He says Susanna has been acting very weirdly lately. And they have been having trouble after trouble with Porter, my great grandson. Derek says that Porter and his mom never get along. They are always yelling at each other. Porter never wants to talk to his dad, because Derek is so '... passive about everything. He always gives in to mom. He never takes a stand.'"

20

"Porter is almost sixteen years old now, with a few months to go. Ever since junior high school, he has hung around with the skateboard crowd; wearing baggy low pocket pants; wearing a baseball cap diagonally over his 'need-a-haircut hair,' and now; has an earring in his left earlobe. His grades have been atrociously low because he never does his homework. However, on general knowledge tests, he always scores highly. He's simply a rebellious youngster headed in the wrong direction; I even think it's toward destruction. He is constantly being 'yelled at' by his mother. And his dad, Derek, doesn't have the courage to ever say anything. Derek simply does not know what to do. Porter has continually been accused of cheating on school tests, shows up late for classes, skips classes, and simply hangs out with his sidewalk skateboard friends who smoke, cuss, and invent new problems to be dealt with. Derek says that Porter is basically a good kid, who has just followed the wrong crowd."

"Before you read this letter, I want you to know that this is basically a summation of the past few weeks of conversations." Quentin handed Ryan the letter from Derek.

"Dear Grandpa Quentin..."

As we discussed extensively on the phone, I want to formally apologize to you for the way Susanna and I treated you in regards to your offer of a free cabin to us. All the improvements suggested were from Susanna's mindset.

Unfortunately, I have never been able to stand up to her. She always overpowers me, and the worst thing is ... that I let her do it. I always try to pacify her desires and I hate any kind of confrontation. I saw how my own Dad was mean, cynical, and always angry. If enough time went by, I always figured that everything would soon pass. But this has not happened with Susanna, or with my son. Now I feel I have to take a stand. I am taking a stand. This letter has to do with my son, Porter.

He has continually gotten into trouble more and more often. I'm ashamed to admit that he is in trouble now... with a second sentencing decision court date set for May 15. I'm not going to go into detail on what happened. He is facing jail time, maybe for six months or more. His mother refuses to talk with him. My son refuses to talk with me.

At the first sentencing hearing, the Judge asked me in court, "Do you, the father, have anything to say or offer before I pass sentence on Porter?"

'Yes, Judge, I have an idea, but I need to think about it some, before I can tell you. I need to check some other details. I like having a son, but I am fed up with his behavior. I know he is smart. I just don't know how to handle him. I know this is an unusual request, but could I possibly have a little more time?"

The judge held some papers in her hand. "From all his general test scores, I notice here that he is a very bright boy, but he's flunking all his classes. I sense that jail might not be the correct answer for him." Judge Sanderson was a large round-faced white-haired black woman with deep compassion in her eyes. She had many years of working with troubled teenagers. "Very well, if you can come up with a plan that will get Porter back into the world of responsibility for his actions, I will listen to it. Court is set for May 29 for final hearing. Porter, young man, you had better listen to your dad. He seems to be the only person standing up for you. He loves you. He just doesn't show it well. Listen to him."

"Grandpa, I always enjoyed our conversations and time up at the cabin. It was always a peaceful time. I always felt recharged in my soul after being up there. I know you have given the use of the cabin to your friend, Ryan Downing, the author. I know he spends most of the summers at the cabin and goes fishing a lot. I have read all of Mr. Downing's 'Peace' books you have passed on to me. For Porter, I think a summer at the cabin with Mr. Downing, fishing, hiking, and peace, could make a difference, a positive difference. I know I don't have any right to ask this, but could you ask Mr. Downing if Porter could spend the summer with him up at the cabin?"

"I have to present a valid plan for the judge, or else, like I said, Porter faces a jail term. Porter is really not a bad kid. He just took to running with the wrong crowd. When you get to know him, he is a fairly decent person, and believe it or not, can be very responsible when he wants to be. We, Susanna and I, have not done a good job of raising him. That's mostly my fault, for not standing up, and I admit it now. Someone has to stand up for my son, and now, that's me. I hope it's not too late."

"I have already talked to the judge. She is also a reader fan of Mr. Downing's 'Pursuit of Peace' books. He is one of her favorite authors. She has tentatively agreed that she would withhold Porter's sentencing for reconsideration, for two weeks, assuming that Mr. Downing would be agreeable to this arrangement."

The judge made the statement, "I don't know if anyone would be willing to take on a troubled teenager whom they don't know."

"I'm just going on a hope and a prayer that the cabin experience would work out. I'm desperate. Could you ask Mr. Downing for me? I need to know as soon as possible, so I can write up the plan for the Judge. Otherwise, I just don't know what to do."

Derek

A second letter was folded behind Quentin's letter. The letter was addressed to Ryan.

"Dear Mr. Downing,

I know this is a lot to ask, and you don't even know me. Grandpa Quentin and I have talked extensively about you over these last few years and months. I have read your books, and I know you have an insight on living a God-

24

guided fulfilled life. Your principles, as stated in your books, have started me out on the pursuit of living that same kind of life. I am starting to go to a businessmen bible study. I'm just beginning to learn about prayer. I am praying for my son, Porter. I think you and the cabin can help him at this crucial time. Grandpa says that you are the type person who might help out. Can you help my son, Porter?"

"The judge said she would give you the authority you need to help with Porter. She is actually bending over backwards to help my son. She evidently sees some good in him. I know, deep inside me, that he is a good boy. I know I have let him down. I will also give definite instructions to my son so that he will not be rebellious or become a burden to you. I just think that peace and quiet in a mountain setting, a little fishing, and being with a person who writes about peace, would be the best therapy he could get at this time of his life."

Thank you for your consideration,

Derek Paisley.

"Anyway, Ryan," said Quentin, "That's the situation. I would ask that you think deep and hard about this. I want you to pray about it, too. I know you will. This is a huge step for anyone to take. I just hope we can somehow save my great grandson. I'm amazed how Derek is finally standing up for something."

"Wow," said Ryan. "This sounds like a big challenge."

He sipped his ice water. He sipped his coffee. He was thinking in his mind. He was simultaneously praying and processing his thoughts. "After all, the cabin was a huge gift to me... Am I thankful for the gift? ...Can I really help a troubled teenager? ... What would you have me do, God?"

Quentin was quiet, too.

The muffled sound of shuffling dishes and clinking silverware blended in with the subdued conversations of the restaurant guests. Ryan wondered how many important conversations were transpiring all at the same time.

"More coffee?" interjected the waitress.

"Yes, thank you," he replied.

"More tea, sir?" the waitress asked Quentin.

"No, I'm fine. Thanks."

Another quiet time transpired between the two old friends. Neither of them spoke. Several minutes silently passed.

"OK..." said Ryan... in a deliberate tone. "Tell Derek I'll do it! Call Derek today and tell him to send me his plan to present to the Judge. If she needs my signature or whatever, just send it to me."

Quentin smiled. Ryan smiled.

# Chapter 2

On May 29, 2009, Judge Olivia Brown handed down her decision.

"Porter Paisley?"

"Yes..."

"Stand up, young man." Porter stood up solemnly, but with a slight slouch, as if standing on one foot.

"Stand up straight!" Porter stiffened and pulled in his shoulders. He added seemingly another inch to his five feet ten inches tall slender body frame. He was dressed in a new suit that his dad had purchased for him and forced him to wear. He wore a dark blue tie and a matching long-sleeved blue dress shirt. His shoes were new. He had a recent haircut that displayed his autumn hazel and brown eyes. The earring in his left ear lobe glittered as he moved his head from side to side. Porter was obviously uncomfortable, worried, and unsure about this "whole court thing." He actually looked strikingly handsome. Porter had looked at himself in the mirror this morning and hardly recognized the nicely dressed young man, almost grown, who was staring back at him.

Judge Brown continued. "I have here in my hand, a letter from your dad, and a letter of agreement from Mr. Ryan Downing, regarding your sentence for the crime you have committed. I have a lot of respect for someone like Mr. Downing, who will step forward and try to help out a troubled teenager, someone he doesn't even know, especially someone like you who has been nothing but trouble and aggravation to all your parents, peers, teachers, elders, and anyone else who has tried to help you. Your record as a teenager is far from good! All the reports indicate that we should give up on you and simply put you in jail before you do even more serious wrongs. For some strange reason, I don't want to do that for you, Porter. I'm going to leave you in the community, on a temporary trial basis. I think you should experience real life on the good side, away from your buddies who you say, 'drag you down all the time.' I say, it's time for you to shape up and straighten up, now! Do you hear what I am saying? Do you understand what I am telling you?"

"Uh...yes," replied Porter softly. He was totally scared.

"I am delaying your final sentencing decision until August 17, 2009. That's about twelve weeks away. I am issuing a temporary parental custody order to Mr. Downing, giving him authority to act in lieu of parental supervision. The order has been signed by both your dad, and your mother." Porter's eyes bulged forward and he glanced back at his mother sitting in the courtroom. She was crying, his dad's arm around her shoulders. Tears were also in his dad's eyes.

"You are to use that three months, Porter, to get your life back together, find out about responsibility, and learn how to care for others. How you do all that is up to you. You will have to make your own decisions. Your actions and decisions will all be of your own choosing. During this time of 'peace retreat,' I will be expecting you to write two different dissertation letters, one letter to Mr. Downing to show appreciation for what he is doing for you, and one to me, indicating that you have changed into a responsible person who shouldn't be sent to jail. If you fail to write these letters, acceptable to me, or try to get by with a simple one-page explanation rather than a well-thought out proposal, then you will definitely go to jail. Just like in Monopoly, 'Go to Jail. Go directly to Jail.' Your dad will deliver you to Mr. Downing's cabin in Colorado on or before June 15, 2009. You will remain under Mr. Downing's jurisdiction until Aug 15, 2009. Do you understand these terms, Porter?"

"Uh..uh... yes..." replied Porter in an almost hushed whisper.

"Speak up!" demanded the Judge.

"Yes. I understand..."

"There are more behavior details outlined in the court order, mostly from your dad, some from me, and some from Mr. Downing. I assure you, Porter, that it's your obligation to begin correcting these flaws in your character. You are now temporarily released to the care of your family. Do you have any questions?"

Almost boldly, Porter replied faintly, "How do I know what to write that will be acceptable to you?"

"That's your decision, Porter. You got here to juvenile court all on your own because of all the decisions you have made so far. You are accustomed to making decisions all by yourself. You have gone the wrong way for some time now. Your decisions, I repeat...your decisions... have delivered you to this courtroom. This will be an opportunity for you to change from making those previous bad decisions... to making some positive choices... and good decisions. It's your choice. I'm giving you a chance to change. You are lucky to be in my courtroom. Not everyone gets a second chance. I see some potential here. So does your dad. Your dad is giving you this second chance. Do you agree to accept all these terms?"

"Yes."

"All right. Before you leave today, you will also place your signature on the behavior details outlined in this court order. I strongly suggest that you follow the order. Do you still agree?"

"Yes"

"So ordered! Court dismissed!"

During Judge Brown's court session, Ryan sat discreetly on the back row of the court benches. He had flown down to Tampa, Florida to visit with Derek about Porter. It was a coincidence that he had a "Pursuit of Peace" speaking engagement two days earlier at a church in Brooksville, Florida, about an hour away. There were several spectators in the courtroom listening to the

30

proceedings. Ryan got up quickly and left quietly. He headed to the airport to catch his plane. Now, it was back to the cabin. Now, in his mind, he had to prepare for this new experience... and his new teenager visitor.

Porter had not met Mr. Downing, and was not aware of who he was. All Porter understood was that he was being "banished into the cold wilderness," somewhere in Colorado, away from Florida. "Everybody was against him. Life wasn't fair. He didn't deserve to be treated this way. It wasn't even my fault!" muttered Porter under his breath as he walked out of the courtroom, head down, counting the floor tiles in the hallway.

# Chapter 3

The airplane ride from Tampa, Florida, to Denver was smooth riding until Porter could see the mountains of Colorado out the window seat. The mountain peaks were still white-capped with snow. The wind suddenly started rocking the airplane, wobbling the plane like a wind-up toy. This was the first time for Porter, to be flying off somewhere. Derek sat in the center seat beside Porter's window seat. The conversation between dad and son had been very minimal and quiet so far. The seatbelt light came on with a, "Ping..." The captain announced over the intercom, "Ladies and gentlemen, we would ask you to fasten your seatbelts and remain in your seats. We will be experiencing some mild turbulence for a little while. We will be climbing to a higher altitude until we approach Denver in about 35 minutes. Thank you."

The plane seemed to be bumping along a bumpy dirt road. Porter turned and asked his dad, "What does that mean?"

"Don't worry about it, son. This is normal for airplanes, even for this 747. I remember the first time I got bounced around. I was the only person who seemed to be scared. Everyone just kept on reading their newspaper and talking, just like it was a normal event. It just made me aware and appreciative of how strong wind and nature can be."

"Oh," said Porter.

Porter felt uncomfortable in his new clothes that he had been forced to wear. Even his new "Nike" sneakers seemed too tight on his feet. His new shirt rubbed the collar of his neck. The new jeans seemed abrasive on his knees. Porter felt trapped and confined in his seat. There wasn't much he could do about his situation. Porter thought about the, "...cave in the mountains" he was being banished to. "Why can't everyone just leave me alone?"

Porter asked, "How long does it take to get to Mr. Downing's cabin?"

"We land in Denver, and pick up our rental car at the airport. Then we drive an hour north to Fort Collins. From there, the cabin is about an hour's drive through the mountains...so a little over two hours driving time."

"Will we be getting something to eat soon? I'm getting hungry."

"Yes, I figure we will stop at a Cracker Barrel Restaurant just outside of Loveland, off the Interstate."

"Will we be stopping and seeing Grandpa Quentin?" Porter asked.

"No. We will be driving straight through to the cabin. Mr. Downing is waiting for me to deliver you this afternoon, late. I'll just be dropping you off and then returning to Fort Collins. Grandpa Quentin and I will have a late supper. I'm staying at his place for a couple of days, before flying back home," replied Derek. "When I come back to get you in

August, Grandpa Quentin wants us to stay for a few days. He's not doing well, health-wise. He might not even make it."

"What do you mean, '...not even make it'?" asked Porter.

"Porter, your Great Grandpa is almost ready to die... almost any time. He's on Hospice care right now. He does want to see and meet and talk to you. He told me that. I know you have never met him, but he's the one who helped set up this mountain cabin visit for you."

"Visit?" replied Porter, sarcastically sharp in his voice. "...being banished into a cave in the mountains... where there's no connection to the world...where none of my friends are... with nothing to do... no communication with my friends... or with anyone in the outside world!"

"Your so-called friends are what got you into this predicament! This is serious, Porter! Whether you realize it or not, this is an undeserved opportunity for you to turn around and become a better person! You have been given a second chance, a gift from out of the blue...I hope you realize that very soon... because if you don't, you will definitely be going to jail."

"I know! I know!" growled Porter. "But why don't I get to choose my own life instead of everyone enforcing their will over me?"

"Well, Porter, let me ask you a question. Do you think you have done a good job with your life so far? As your dad,

34

I think I've done a lousy job of helping you. I have to live with that. You also have to live with that. All we can do now is to make some kind of good course correction... that you are free to make. You can either follow the curve in the road... or drive right off the cliff, if that's what you want to do. This can be an adventure for you, or just another reason to go around getting yourself into trouble and sulking forever."

Derek paused and then continued, "You are to be respectful of Mr. Downing. You are expected to pitch in and help around the cabin. In addition to the two letters you are writing for the Judge, Mr. Downing will also be writing a report to the Judge. Don't try to use fake flattery. Just please learn from this experience. It could be the best summer time you have ever had! This is not punishment. This is an opportunity. I hope and pray for you, regardless of the outcome, but... I will definitely be turning you over to your own decisions. You can be a responsible person in society or you can choose to hobnob in jails from this point on. You will definitely get to choose which way you want to live. I'm tired of your irresponsibility. This is a glorious opportunity, if you choose to take it..."

"Sure... sure..." muttered Porter. In his angry mind, Porter was thinking, "Why is everyone telling me what I can do and cannot do? I can make my own decisions...just leave me alone..."

"You have eight weeks, Porter... better make the best of it!"

Porter wondered in his mind why his dad had now started becoming bold with his statements. "Maybe it's because his mom wasn't there to order him around..."

# Chapter 4

Derek and Porter stopped at the Cracker Barrel Restaurant, just off I-25 at Loveland. They both ordered the chicken fried steak dinner with mashed potatoes and gravy, biscuits, and a hot apple side dish. Father and son sat in silence, with seemingly nothing to say to each other. The huge fireplace flamed brightly, sending out beaming heat surges into the massive, packed, noisy dining room.

Derek picked up the meal check and placed a tip of $2.50 on the table. "Now, Porter, do you understand that you are to give no trouble to Mr. Downing?"

"Yes, Dad, we have been over this a hundred times... I will be your model citizen...OK? I really don't have a choice, do I? I'm being forced into acting like I enjoy this imprisonment... in a sense; it will be like jail... so many restrictions... it's just not fair!"

"Guess what, Porter, life isn't fair! Is it fair that you have become a burden to me and to your mother? Do you think I enjoy having to turn you over to someone else to regain some peace in my life? Do you ever care about someone else other than yourself? This attitude you have, 'stinks,' and I'm tired of it! Yes, life isn't fair. It's not fair for me, either. Other than loving you, I can't see much reason for having you around. I know that you want to get away from our family as soon as possible. I just want you to have somewhat of a good life, grow up normally, have a family, and become somebody. Just ask yourself one question... would you, as a father, want to have a son like you?"

Porter didn't reply.

"Let's get going. Porter. We have about an hour and a half driving."

In his thoughts, Porter pondered, "Why is Dad speaking so strongly to me? He has never done that before. He is just being mean, just like Mom. Now, they are both against me. I can't ever do anything right. Might as well be in jail... then I could get away from it all..."

It was about 2:00 PM, Colorado time, when they turned their rental car onto Highway 14. They headed up Poudre Canyon, past Laporte, following the winding road beside the meandering channel of the Poudre River. They soon found themselves immediately enveloped into the splendor of the majestic mountains. No conversation transpired. Father and son proceeded silently through the canyon. The mountain splendor and twisting river canyon seemed to offer a peaceful free enveloping welcome.

Porter modestly spoke up, "Are there fish in that river?"

"Yes."

"What kind?"

"I think Rainbow trout. I usually caught Brook trout when I was up here before. Mr. Downing probably knows. There is a stream and a lake on his property. You can ask him."

"I don't like fishing. I can't see any point in it."

They continued in silent journey until they came to the turnoff road that led up to Ryan's cabin. The gate was open. The cabin was located about a half-mile off the main road. As they bounced along the old logging road, Porter grew more apprehensive about this enforced venture. It seemed like all the forces of nature were against him. The pressure he felt, gnawed away at his stomach. The fear of the unknown crept crawling steadily into his mind and being. "How could his dad... and mom... do this to him? Who was this stranger he was going to have to suffer and live with for two months? He must be way too old! It doesn't even sound like he has a television set. Why am I losing out on my summer time?"

"Now you understand, Porter, what your restrictions are. You are to be no trouble to Mr. Downing! You are a guest at his cabin, his home, and his rules... I want you to show respect, appreciation... and get along. I won't be coming back for you until August. You are on your own, now, and you need to learn how to behave, starting now... Do you understand?"

"Yes, Dad." Quit bugging me. I know the rules... we have been over this already..."

The rental car popped out into the clearing where the cabin was nestled. Ryan was sitting on the screened-in porch. Derek guided the car up in front of the porch. Derek and Ryan shook hands. "Good to see you, Derek."

"Ryan, this is my son, Porter."

"Welcome, Porter," said Ryan, extending his hand. Porter put his hand limply into Ryan's firm grip.

"Hi," gestured Porter.

"Your room is the first bedroom on the left. You can put all your stuff in there. Do you want some help unloading your gear?"

"No, I can get it."

"OK."

"Where is your bathroom?" asked Porter.

"Down at the end of the hall between the two bedrooms. It's a little tight quarters but it suffices."

"Derek, would you like a cup of coffee, or a cold drink?"

"Do you have a Pepsi? That sounds good."

"Sure, come and sit on the porch. I will bring it out to you. That sounds good to me... too. Do you want ice or cold out of the can?"

"Ice would be fine."

Ryan and Derek sat on the porch, drinking the iced root beer and Pepsi.

"I remember the peaceful serenity of this porch," reflected Derek. "It's amazing how it's so easy to forget the feeling. Working and watching television just somehow doesn't even partially compare. I sure hope Porter doesn't give you trouble, Mr. Downing. He knows he is here under observation, but I really don't know my own son very well.

40

I'm not sure what his reactions will be. It's really great that you are doing this for him... and me."

"Well," said Ryan, "Growing up, my own family life wasn't that great. No one in my family cared about each other. We all just sort of, existed, really. So, I might understand a little bit where Porter is coming from. But it's easy to accept the peace of this mountain cabin, once you get used to it. It takes a while to get used to the slower pace of living. I think we can manage together, at least for these next two months. I don't think I could handle a teenager in the city. There would be too many distractions. How does Porter feel about everything?"

"He's still angry," replied Derek. "He's still rebelling towards any kind of authority. He hasn't learned to care for anyone else but himself. He's still raw about growing up. It's like he has one foot in youth and one foot straddled on adulthood."

Porter opened the screen door and came onto the porch.

"Want a Pepsi or something cold to drink?" asked Ryan.

"Sure."

"Help yourself to the refrigerator, Porter. Get whatever you want." Porter returned with a cold can of Sprite. He leaned back on the half-wall of the screened in porch. The three visited for about five minutes.

"Porter," Derek said, "Better get the rest of your things out of the trunk. I have to leave now to go meet Grandpa Quentin."

"OK."

Porter set out the two suitcases on the ground.

"I'll pick you up in two months, OK?"

Porter didn't say anything. He just picked up the two suitcases and took them inside to the bedroom that Mr. Downing had told him was Porter's.

"Thanks again, for doing this, Mr. Downing. I gave Porter some money for spending cash. Here is an envelope for you, with money for you to help with the groceries and anything else Porter might need. He knows all about the rules for staying here. Like I said, I don't know how he will respond. He's still angry. He's still growing up. This will be a vacation away from his mother. Call me if he becomes too big a problem."

"We'll just be patient and let him adjust as we go," said Ryan. "Don't worry. A week or two of fishing will probably help him more than anything."

"He told me on the way up that he didn't like to fish."

Porter reentered the porch with another Sprite can in his hand.

"See you, son."

"See you, Dad."

Dad & son gave each other a hug. It was easy to tell that not much affection was shared very often. It was a stilted hug.

Ryan and Porter stood together and watched the rental car disappear through the trees. Old man and young boy stood on the porch, sipping their drinks. "Welcome, Porter. Glad to have you here. Have a seat. Let's enjoy this warm sunny afternoon."

The two strangers sat and sipped, acquiescing to their situation. Warm spring air wafted through the porch. A quiet agitation seemingly crept onto the porch. He glanced over towards the restless teenager, who was now his guest. Porter slouched in his chair with his baseball cap turned backwards over his neck. His slender angling frame resembled a small bulging aspen tree. Porter had narrow arms that protruded lazily from his body. He had a clear complexion that didn't show any tanning of his skin. Both strangers sat in silence, as if in different worlds.

Ryan picked up the book he had been reading and flipped to where he left off. The book he was reading was one of the Pursuit of Peace books he had authored. He read his own books to keep himself motivated and guided on the right path. Over an hour passed with no conversation. He glanced over at Porter several times and then continued reading his book. Porter just sat and sipped on his second can of Sprite, staring into the open clearing, seemingly oblivious to his situation. The stalemate quietness suddenly broke.

"So... what am I supposed to do here? Am I supposed to work for you, or what? What do I have to do to get a good write-up from you? I hear you are supposed to write me up for whatever is wrong with me."

Ryan placed his book on the table beside him. "Well first of all, let's introduce ourselves. You can call me, Mr. Downing, and I will call you, Porter."

"All right, Mr. Downing," he said sarcastically with disdain, "what am I supposed to do here? You know I didn't have a choice to come here. I was ordered to be here, and I'm really not too happy about it."

"Well Porter, that makes two of us. I'm not that happy about having you here, either, especially with that attitude it looks like you already have. I write books on peace. You certainly don't exude peace to me. Since we are both a little unsettled at the moment, let's talk about some accommodation and respect rules."

"More rules? More rules? I already got the message from the judge...no TV, no internet, no video games, no Nintendo, no cell phone, no friends, no nothing; I can't even go into town alone, without you holding my hand... I'm stuck up here with an old man, with absolutely nothing to do."

"Well like it or not, Porter, we both have to coexist for the next two months. Sure, I'm old! So what? I'm stuck here with a young man who is facing a jail sentence. I really

44

don't know what to do or how to interact with you. Don't worry. I'm not going to try to be a father to you or try to hold your hand. I'm going to treat you like an adult, that is, if you can handle it. You already have me riled up and I'm simply going to attempt to make that obnoxious feeling dissipate more and more. I'm just as human and emotional as you are, so you better get used to it."

Ryan managed to keep his cool... even though inside, he was seething. He was amazed at how easily he flew off the handle with anger towards this young man he really didn't know. "How come attitudes can be so contagious?" he thought, "and why do the negative vibes surface so easily? Come on now, Ryan, you have been around lots of life situations that have upset you. Are you going to let this kid get to you? Aren't you the person who writes about peace? Simmer down...let's turn this sour lemon situation into lemonade..."

Porter didn't expect this type of outburst... he had to sit back. Reluctantly he listened.

Calmly, Mr. Downing laid out the guidelines for coexistence.

"First, whoever cooks, washes the dishes, and cleans up the kitchen. We take turns cooking. No dirty dishes left in the sink. No clothes lying around. The cabin is picked up and kept neat as we go. Your one primary chore is to keep the firewood bins full."

"As you said, you have no access to the Internet. I have had my friend, Nathan, set up a password path that will not allow you to access the Internet or any of my computers. You have no cell phone privileges. You will be able to access a Microsoft Word program when you want to get around to writing your letters. There is no television. I like to watch movies. You can watch any of the movies any time you want, except when I am writing. I like it quiet when I am composing. I do most of my writing early in the mornings, so most of the day is available to you. I do like to go fishing, often. You are welcome to go with me. I have extra fishing gear." Mr. Downing continued, "I like to go down in the canyon to a restaurant for breakfast. You are welcome to come with me. I will buy your breakfast if you come. Your dad gave us grocery money for meals here at the cabin. You can help plan and grocery shop and pick up food for the meals."

"I don't know how to cook..." replied Porter.

"You'll learn."

"What do I do during the day?"

"Enjoy the scenery."

"I've already seen it," replied Porter. "What is there to do all week long?"

"Think of this time as a vacation, a time to slow down and think, a time to relax and reflect. Think of this time as making a plan for the future. It will take a little while, to get used to the outdoors, but it will happen. I also have books that you are welcome to read."

"Well, it all seems very boring to me."

"As I said before, you are also welcome to use my fishing equipment. There's a lot of good fishing around here, the stream, the lake..."

"I don't like fishing!"

"OK, Porter. Have it your way. How about having hamburgers on the grill tonight for supper?"

Porter grunted a muffled reply. Ryan returned to his book. Silence again enveloped the porch.

# Chapter 5

Porter got up and shuffled off the porch. The late afternoon sun was intensifying its control of the sprawling forest below. Ryan remained in the shade on the porch. He observed Porter walking around the clearing. Porter's head was down, his eyes looking at his feet, scuffling in the dust of the clearing. His slouching slender frame reminded Ryan of limp single spaghetti noodle hanging over the edge of a bowl. It was very obvious that Porter was not happy with his surroundings or with the events now being forced upon him. Ryan wondered in his mind why he had agreed to this "unique" proposal with this young man, even if it had appeared to be something he could do for God ... and for Quentin. Ryan muttered a prayer in his mind, "Lord, show me what to do and be. I really need all the help I can get."

Ryan continued his reading. The restless teenager walked around the clearing three times. On the fourth lap, on the other side of the clearing, he stopped and disappeared into the pine trees. Ryan could hear the squirrels barking their incessant chatter. As if annoyed, blue jays flew up from the branches making what sounded to Ryan like grunting sounds. Ryan was accustomed to listening to the forest. Porter remained out of view for about a half an hour. He reversed his walking direction and ambled back towards the cabin porch.

It was now about 5:30, Ryan guessed. "Ready for some supper, Porter?"

"Sure," replied Porter, glancing up at Ryan.

"Want some hamburgers?"

"I guess... OK." replied Porter.

"How about you fix the burgers and I'll take care of the trimmings? The grill is on the side of the cabin. You can bring it out front and you can cook the burgers over by the corner of the porch, over there," said Ryan, pointing with his finger.

"I don't know how to cook. I've never cooked in my life! I told you!" exclaimed Porter.

"No time to learn like now. The charcoal is in a bag in the kitchen pantry beside the refrigerator. Bring out the can of charcoal lighter fluid, too. Fill up the grill about one third in a pile."

Porter followed instructions and went in to the kitchen. He returned to the porch with the charcoal and lighter fuel can. "Now, what do I do?"

"Pull that Weber black charcoal grill up by the corner of the porch. Lift up that round lid. Take off the round grill insert and place the charcoal in a pile underneath, like a mound. Fill it up about one third full. Open the lever on the bottom so air can get in."

"Now what?"

"Squirt the lighter fluid over the briquettes. Let the fluid soak in for a little bit. There are some stick matches in the kitchen cupboard. Go and get some."

"I have a lighter in my pocket. I can use that."

"I don't think that would be a good idea. The hair on your knuckles and arm might go up in flames. Better use the matches... and stand back."

Porter returned and threw in a flaring match. The charcoal lighter fluid popped and immediately started spewing up flames and smoke.

"The flames will go down after a little bit." said Ryan. "The charcoal will take a while to get hot, probably in about half an hour. You can tell when the coals are ready. They turn ashen gray and start glowing red. That's when you can start cooking. Why don't you go and get the hamburgers ready, I'll whip up a salad and slice some tomatoes."

"I told you I don't know how to cook or fix hamburgers!"

Ryan was amazed in his mind that this young man had never cooked a hamburger before. "Just open the refrigerator and pull out the one pound package of hamburger. Then on the countertop, just make four patties with your hands, all about the same size and put them on a paper plate. Use a pancake turner."

The old man started creating a salad with lettuce, green onions and chopped-up tomatoes, topped off with some shredded sharp Colby yellow cheddar cheese. He diced up a polish style dill pickle. The young man started molding the round hamburger piles.

"How do I get the piles to be patties?"

"Just use the heel of your hand and then shape them a little bit."

"When do I put them on the grill?"

"Go out and check the coals. They probably aren't ready yet. Want some music? See if you can find a CD you might like, and play it on the CD player. I like to listen to music when I'm preparing a meal."

Porter checked the coals. "No, there's no heat coming off."

Porter started reviewing Mr. Downing's CD collection. He selected a "Tchaikovsky" CD and turned up the volume. The cabin bulged with the sound of a full orchestra playing. Ryan recognized the tune of the "1812 Overture."

"Let's have supper out on the porch. You like pork and beans out of a can?"

"Nope."

"Ok, I'm not supposed to eat beans either."

"We'll eat on the tables beside the chairs. We can set all the trimmings on the round table. Do you want milk, juice, or pop?"

"Pop. Pepsi."

Ryan began carrying out the mustard, relish, ketchup, onions, cheese, and salad, and hamburger buns.

He brought out the Light Balsamic and Basil Vinaigrette salad dressing, two disposable plastic salad bowls, a bag of Lay's Baked Potato Chips, and a medium sized jar of medium-hot Pace salsa. The stilled wind suddenly started swirling. Ryan had to make sure all the paper plates and napkins were anchored down with a bottle of ketchup or mustard. The paper cups blew off the table and Ryan retrieved them before they scooted off the porch. The wind fanned the glowing charcoal coals. The coals were turning white on the edges. Soon the odor of charcoal started permeating the mountain air. He relished these times of solitude and peace.

"Tchaikovsky" boomed from inside the cabin to flood the porch with classical music melodies. Porter was trying to figure out how to get the hamburgers on the grill.

"Spread out the coals with a stick. Use the long bar-b-que fork to place that round grill screen inside the grill. You can use that long spatula on the side of the grill to put the hamburgers on. You can put the lid on while they cook."

"How will I know when they are done?" asked Porter.

"You will be able to tell. If they turn out all black, you cooked them too long." Ryan smiled at his statement. "Here, why don't you sprinkle the burgers with some Montreal Steak Seasoning and some garlic powder? After you flip over the burgers, we can put the cheese on top. Also, I like to warm up the buns on the grill."

Finally, the hamburgers were done. He and Porter sat quietly, the wind subsiding again. Porter was hungry and downed his two hamburgers quickly, along with four handfuls of potato chips. "You want another hamburger? I'm only supposed to eat one. Want some salad?"

"OK." Porter consumed the remaining burger. He toyed with the salad, but still managed to eat most of it. He poured on a tiny portion of the Balsamic dressing. He picked with his fork and pushed the pickles to the side. "I don't think I like pickles."

The cabin music wafted out onto the porch, filling the forest with strange and mysterious melodies. The old man and the young man again sat in quiet acquiescence. Pine tree fragrances filled the porch as the sun started creeping down the horizon in back of the cabin. Ryan brought out a Coleman lantern. Soon the mantle glowed and started producing heat and light. Bugs started hovering and bumping into the light. "Want some apple pie for dessert? We can get a fire going in the fireplace. I like to have coffee and dessert by the fire."

"What about the coals in the grill?" asked Porter.

"We can just let them go out on their own. Just put the lid on and let them burn out. Oh, if you want to roast some marshmallows, there are some in the cupboard on the right of the sink. The grill heat is still there."

A small moment of time passed.

"Well, I would say that you cooked a good first meal, wouldn't you, Porter?"

"I still don't know how to cook," replied Porter.

"How about watching a movie on the DVD player?" I thought we would watch, 'The Bridge on the River Kwai.' It's one of my favorites." Porter remained unspoken and emotionless.

Ryan paused for a moment and then spoke. "I'm going to have breakfast at the Mountain Greenery Resort Café in the morning. They open at 7:00 so I will be leaving about twenty minutes till seven. I'll buy your breakfast if you want to come along."

"I can pay for my own breakfast!" growled Porter. "I have my own money." Porter paused in his thoughts... "I don't see any clocks around and you don't even wear a watch. How do you know when it's time to get up?"

The morning wakes me up. I have a built-in awareness of the time of day. I've practiced it for a long time. You will learn to do the same, if you want. I can usually guess the time within 10 or 15 minutes. I see you don't have a watch, either. Did you bring an alarm clock?"

"No."

"That's good. I'm going inside to fix myself a cup of coffee with my pie. I'll start the fire. You can wash the dishes."

# Chapter 6

Ryan entered the Mountain Greenery Restaurant. Sharon greeted him. "Good morning, Ryan. How are you doing this bright and glorious morning?"

"Hi Sharon, I'm doing very well, thank you."

Sharon had a friendly smile and long sleek blonde hair that draped over her shoulders and cascaded half-way down her back. She had a habit of inadvertently winking at everybody with her left eye. The gesture and smile combination always made everyone feel welcome. Her congenial and friendly manner affected everyone in an upbeat way. Porter had remained in bed back at the cabin, choosing not to go to the restaurant.

"Coffee?"

"Yes, and a glass of ice water."

"Do you need a menu?"

"No, I know what I like."

"Want your usual then? 'Farmer's Son?' Wheat toast? Scrambled eggs?"

"Yes... where's Vic?"

"Oh, he's out putting lids on the trash cans. We had a visit from a bear last night."

"Really?" What happened?"

"Mary Lucas, one of the residents, called me and said she heard something about 3:30 this morning. She said she saw a black blob moving around in the dark around the garbage cans. She couldn't quite make out the silhouette. Vic said it was definitely a bear. I forget. You want cream for your coffee?"

"No, black is fine."

Sharon poured coffee into the thick durable porcelain mug. She took his order ticket to the kitchen and placed it on the circular order holder. Above the kitchen grill window, was a chalkboard with a new saying written on it. Ryan enjoyed the encouragements and pondering thoughts that were displayed on a daily basis. Today's message was, "Enjoy today, yesterday is already gone."

"Are you in charge of the sayings that go on that chalkboard, Sharon?"

"Yes, I get a lot of good comments from people who come in... and I really enjoy doing it."

He really valued having breakfast at this small restaurant in the mountains. Vic and Sharon operated this restaurant as part of the cabin and RV park facility. Many local canyon residents lived in the area in year-round cabins. Lots of good old mountain folks and travelers were regular customers. To Ryan, it seemed like almost everyone who came in, knew each other. In addition, lots of family tourists came in for vacation meals. The restaurant layout was unique. The restaurant had been remodeled several times over the previous years. At the west end, Vic had his little fishing supply store. He also operated his real estate office from there. The restrooms were small and tight, with the names "Bucks" and "Does" displayed above the names "Gentlemen" and "Ladies." Sharon was in charge of the tourist gift shop that occupied the front part of the rustic former old cabin. A wooden bear carved out of a log stood silently by the door. When Ryan's books were in booklet form, Sharon had displayed and sold some of Ryan's original booklets.

On the wall opposite the front door, there was a kitchen counter with five stools. The kitchen was behind. On the left, just inside the front door, was a full seating booth beside the cash register. The store area opened into a large room that obviously been added at a later date. There were about seven booths on the north side and three booths on the south side. For large gatherings, four small tables were pushed together to make a large long table in the middle of the room. All the leather-looking upholstered booths were cast in an emerald-green color. The windows let the morning sunshine gleam in. The sun-bright dining room blushed with green effervescence. A sliding patio door opened out onto a patio area with wrought iron tables and chairs. Towards the river, beyond the patio, was an open park with picnic tables. Like today, when the weather was warm and nice, with the patio door open, Ryan could hear the river water rushing by, full of late spring and early summer runoff. He often took a stroll by the river after breakfast. He enjoyed the peaceful majesty of this mountain setting.

The Patio door was open. Bird melodies lingered in the air. From the feeders hanging outside the windows, multi-adorned, vibrant rainbow-colored hummingbirds hovered and sipped the red sugar water. At the far end of this new addition was an almost separate family room living area with soft sofas, coffee table, chairs, lamps, and a flagstone fireplace. Board games, chess and checker sets, and puzzles lay upon the coffee table. After hours, this was definitely a family gathering place. The restaurant was open from 7:00 to 2:00.

The screen door jingled open. Vic came strolling in.

"Hi, Ryan."

"Hi, Vic. I hear you have been out chasing bears today!"

"Yeah, they have been visiting us every once in a while. I haven't actually seen them, but Mary, one of our residents, said she heard one last night. She saw a black blob early this morning but couldn't really tell in the dark. The bear has been scrounging around the trashcans, making a mess."

"Have you ever seen a bear up here, Vic?"

"No. I never have, but I've heard several reports, especially these past few years." Vic poured a cup of coffee for himself and sat down across from Ryan.

"Last week," commented Ryan, "... out of the window here, I saw a red fox trotting down the highway. He had a large bulky bone in his mouth, like a rump of a deer.

58

He looked really exhausted, but he was trotting right down the highway, headed west."

"I think one of the residents has been feeding the fox. That's not a good idea. Well, Ryan, did your new visitor show up Monday?"

"Yep, he did."

"How did it go?" asked Vic.

"Let's just say it was very interesting."

"I thought you were going to bring him in and introduce him."

"He was asleep this morning...sound asleep, so I let him sleep. He didn't want to wake up..."

"Hi, Paulette."

"Hi, Mr. Downing. Want me to top off your coffee?"

"Sure."

Vic and Ryan shared back and forth with what he called, "canyon chatter." More customers started drifting in. Vic said hello to each person and group. He knew by name... just about everybody. Vic table-hopped, greeting each of the new customers and the regulars. He also refilled the coffee cups, often.

"It's neat that you have Paulette here to help you, Vic. I know that it keeps getting really busy for you and Sharon to handle all the time."

"Yeah... it seems like I always end up with having to fix or repair something, somewhere. I never lack for anything to do. It's really hard to get restaurant help up here in the canyon. Paulette just started here a couple of weeks ago. She relates and interacts with customers very easily. She fits in very well. We furnish her a trailer unit to live in and we pay for her meals. It's about the only way we can get anyone to stick around for our whole busy season. She really does help. She's saving up for college next year. She just graduated from high school. Her folks live in Fort Collins. She comes up Wednesday through Sunday and goes home on Mondays and Tuesdays. She has her own car. Sharon needs to go into town today to get supplies, so Paulette is helping out today to fill in for Sharon."

"Yes, replied Ryan, "I was impressed that Paulette remembered my name, after just one introduction. Have you been getting any fishing in, Vic?"

"Yes. Max Shepherd and I fished for a couple of hours yesterday, up by the outlet, downstream from the fish hatchery."

"Did you catch any?"

"We had some strikes, but the river is still fairly full and muddy. Max hooked into one, but the fish got off. I think we will have to wait for the river to go down before the fishing gets good. How's the fishing up at your place?"

"Well I've been doing a lot of writing this past week, and I've been preparing in my mind for this visit from Porter. I haven't got much fishing in yet. I usually hike up the trail beside the stream when I take a break from writing. I just enjoy being in the outdoors."

"Yes, that's why we fish, isn't it?"

"Yes, Vic. It's not about catching fish... it's all about being there... being here... and enjoying the experience."

"You are right about that!"

# Chapter 7

Ryan lingered and visited with some of the restaurant guests, paid for his breakfast, and climbed back into his Jeep. He headed back to the cabin. He guessed that it was probably around 9:30. The cabin was about twenty minutes away. As he approached the clearing in front of the cabin, he saw Porter come around from the side of the porch and quickly sit down on one of the chairs. He seemed to be in a hurry to sit down. Ryan turned off the ignition. He walked up the soft, spongy, but strong steps, and opened the screen door onto the screened-in porch. "Hi, Porter."

"Hi..."

In front of Ryan was a slovenly young man dressed in baggy jeans, long pockets, dirty oversize sneakers, wearing a baseball cap semi-backwards. He was the direct opposite of the neatly dressed young man who had shown up yesterday. Ryan went inside the cabin. On the kitchen table was a half-full bowl of cereal, a half-full carton of orange juice, and an almost empty carton of milk. Cereal was sprawled and scattered all around the bowl. A banana peel, an open bag of bagels, and a spoon lay by the side of the bowl. He sniffed the air in the kitchen. Smoke permeated the cabin. He turned around and went back to the porch where Porter was sitting.

"All right, Porter. Let's have them! "

"Have what?"

"Your cigarettes. I know you have been smoking. The cabin reeks with the smell. You know the rules. No smoking! You even signed your name to the rules. Where is your stash?"

"I only had one cigarette. I smoked it outside."

"You are lying! Where is your stash? Do I have to go in and inspect your luggage and room by myself? Ryan could feel his internal anger rising, like a tremulous volcano. Porter reluctantly stood up. He shuffled to his bedroom. He opened his suitcase and pulled out a white sock. Inside were a handful of cigarettes."

"All of them, Porter!"

From underneath some shirts, Porter reached in and pulled out a half-full Marlborough cigarette carton.

"Is that all of them, Porter?"

"Yeah..."

"Now go into the living room and throw them into the fireplace. We will burn them up tonight. Don't even think about smoking in this cabin again... or anywhere else for the next eight weeks. That's one of the rules you signed your name to."

"I can't stop," whined Porter, "I have to have a smoke now and then. It calms my nerves. Besides, I'm not hurting anybody. It's my choice to do what I want."

"Not while you are my guest! Do you understand the word, 'No,' Porter? No smoking! How many did you smoke today, already? How many?"

Porter looked at his feet, not daring to look at Mr. Downing. "Maybe three or four."

Ryan marched Porter into the living room. "Now throw all the cigarettes into the fireplace. What did you do with the butts you smoked today?"

"I threw them off the porch onto the ground outside."

"You can go outside and pick up every cigarette butt and also throw them into the fireplace. Hand me the lighter."

"The what?"

"Your cigarette lighter in your pocket. You will not need it any longer."

Porter reached into his baggy pocket and reluctantly handed over the Bic lighter. Ryan pointed towards the fireplace. Porter tossed all the cigarette stash on the black ashes left from last night's fire.

"Now Porter, this is your first day here. I have some rules that you will abide by. You already know what they are. I am an easy person to get along with, but I cannot, and will not put up with, your sarcastic attitude and your deliberate breaking of the rules. Did you have breakfast here this morning? Sure you did, look at this mess! You will keep this kitchen clean as we go. I was going to share the cleanup with you, but from now on, it will be your daily chore. No matter who cooks, it will be your job to clean the kitchen after every meal... and keep it clean. You do not leave food out! You will put food away in the refrigerator or the cabinets. You wash the dishes and put them away immediately after every meal. Do you understand, Porter?"

Porter nodded slightly.

"Let's get another thing straight, Porter. What happened to those nice clothes you were wearing yesterday? You look like a pig today. From now on you are to wear respectable looking clothes. And if you wear a ball cap, wear it right and normal. I'll not have you dressing as if you were a member of a sidewalk skateboard clan. You can take out that earring, too. It does nothing for your appearance. Are you going to polish it up before you go to your first job interview?"

"You can't make me take out my earring!"

"Ok, maybe not right now... go in and change clothes. Did you take a shower today?"

"No."

"Around here you take a shower every day. You can take it at night or in the morning. It's your choice. I usually take mine early in the mornings. I think there will be enough hot water for the both of us if we go conservative."

"One other thing, Porter, you are going to have to learn how to get up early in the morning. You can't be sleeping away half the day all the time. I will wake you the first few days so we can go out and have breakfast, but after this week, it's your responsibility to get up. Do you have any questions?"

Porter said nothing.

"Can you make up your bed every day?"

Porter stood there.

"Starting tomorrow, you will make up your bed every day. We wash clothes once a week. You do yours. I do mine. "Ok, do you know what your chores are? Bring in some firewood every day, too... It's your job to keep the fireplace bin full of firewood."

Ryan took a Jonathan apple out of the refrigerator. He walked outside in the clearing and headed for his favorite solitude rock at the edge of the clearing beside the stream. He began pondering, "Does this kid really know the meaning of the word, 'No'? What am I up against?" He sat in the shade and paid attention to the rippling and bubbling stream. He chomped on his shiny red apple.

Porter grumbled as he began cleaning up the kitchen. He was angry, mad, and upset.

"I might as well be in jail. Why does everyone try to boss me around? Why don't they just leave me alone?"

Quickly, the kitchen was somewhat cleaner. The milk and orange juice cartons were back in the refrigerator. Porter used some Ivory dishwashing soap from under the sink to clean the bowls, glasses, and spoon. He even dried the dishes with a red-and-white checkered dishcloth. He noticed that the dishcloth matched the kitchen curtains and the kitchen tablecloth. Porter sprayed some blue Windex cleaner on the countertop and wiped it off. Amazingly, he thought, the kitchen smelled clean.

Porter went to the fireplace and plucked out the Marlborough carton. "Just one... he will never know the difference..." Porter's mind began drifting and justifying another cigarette. He stood for a moment by the fireplace, reconsidering his instinctive decision. After a minute, he threw the carton back into the fireplace. "I better go out and find those butts from this morning or he'll rake me over the coals again." Porter reluctantly discovered all five cigarette butts. As instructed, he also pitched them into the fireplace.

Porter went in and took a steamy hot shower. It felt good. Porter had just begun shaving. He shaved with his Gillette double bladed razor. He even brushed his teeth that had started giving him trouble lately. He retrieved his new clothes from yesterday. The clothes still felt uncomfortable. "I still don't like this..." He put on his ball cap and tried to straighten it towards the front. "This makes me look like a geek." He admired his earring in his left ear. He left his old clothes in a pile on his bed. "I'll make up the bed tomorrow."

He walked around the clearing until he saw Mr. Downing sitting by the stream. He ambled over.

"You look like a new man, Porter. You want to try fishing this afternoon, after lunch?

"No. I don't know how to fish."

"Well I do know how to fish. You can do whatever you want, Porter, but I'm going to follow the stream up to Cascade Pool. I'm going to have a good time. You might want to consider having a good time, too. I'll see you later."

Ryan returned to the cabin, put on his hiking boots, and donned his fishing vest. He put a Jonathan apple and two "Oats n' Honey" granola bars in his vest pocket. He put on his Bluegrass Gospel Jam baseball cap, and grabbed his fly-fishing pole. He started up the trail following the stream. "Who doesn't like fishing?" he thought.

Soon, the cabin disappeared into the background into the forest. The fisherman silently crept along the stream banks. The quiet encircled Ryan. His thoughts emerged like emanating sunbeams of wonder and amazement. He felt at home in this peace-filled serenity setting in God's country. Silently flipping his line into pools of swirling currents, he worked his way upstream. A half-hour transpired before he had his first strike. Every time he fished this stream, even daily, a different pool would open up. Man and nature talked to each other. God and Ryan spoke internally. The warm breeze stood up and caressed Ryan's fly line. Ryan's quiet approach caused the wilderness to accept him as a forest friend. He patiently and stealthily took his time, amongst the willows, crouching and sneaking up on both new and old fishing spots. He stopped and tied on an Adams brown fly pattern. That fly didn't work. Next, he tied on an Adams Parachute fly. Wow! A huge rainbow took the fly and swished through the surface with a huge splash! The fish was gone as quickly as he had spun upward through the surface of the water.

About an hour later, the stream leveled off into a meandering meadow. He had named this spot, "High Mountain Meadow." He walked over to the edge of the meadow and sat in the shade of some green-leafed Aspen trees. He consumed one of the granola bars he had brought along. In addition he had brought along a bottle of water. The forest was buzzing with insect activity. Flies swarmed around Ryan's perspiring brow. They bit Ryan's ankles, right through his white socks. He always wondered how little flies could bite through white socks. He contemplated his surroundings. "Thanks, God. I really appreciate being out here enjoying what you have provided. These mountains are a marvelous demonstration of how you put this world together. And I get to enjoy it."

His thoughts traced back to the young man back at the cabin. "Maybe Porter needs some time of solitude, too." Ryan dozed peacefully in the shade.

# Chapter 8

Porter watched Mr. Downing start his hike up the stream. Porter went up to the porch and sat in one of the rocking chairs. He was bored. There was nothing to do. Porter sniffed the air. "Smells like a skunk or a dead raccoon." Porter went inside and found another can of Sprite in the refrigerator. He pulled on the tab and sipped the cold carbonated soda. "I wonder what this old guy does when there's nothing to do."

He took a look around his new "jail cell." On the wall beside the entrance door was a whole wall of family pictures. Mr. Downing wasn't in most of the pictures. The photos mostly consisted of young kids. Some of the pictures showed the same young kids holding up fish they had caught. Other photos showed the young kids with music instruments. Hung on the other walls, were large pictures of mountain cabins, usually situated by a lake or mountain stream. The kitchen had a breakfast bar with three wooden stools. Two black skillets and two large copper-bottom cooking pots hung from the log ceiling beams. Next to the kitchen bar was a wooden table with a vise attached to the side. Packages of feathers lay in the corner. Spools of different colored threads sat by bottles of glue and coiled thin nylon line. A brightly adorned book was on the table, with the title, "Fly Fishing Patterns for Colorado."

To the right, in the far corner of the living room were two walls of shelves, filled with books, like a library. The flagstone fireplace was located in the center of the wall. Firewood was piled on each end of the fireplace. The hearth area had a semi-circle stone spark inhibitor surrounding the base of the fireplace. In the right corner of the room, away from the fireplace, several musical instruments stood on individual stands. There were two guitars, a violin, an electric bass, a pear-shaped small instrument, a well-worn banjo, and a large old piano. There were four padded stools. Four padded folding chairs were folded and leaned upon the wall. Below the window overlooking the porch, were two Dell computers on a desk, one stand up box computer, and a laptop. The CD player sat next to the writing desk, on the far right side.

In the center of the room, to the left of the fireplace, Porter saw that the DVD player was located under the TV screen. In front of the fireplace was circled a sofa and two stuffed leather reclining chairs. Two lamps with green ceramic bases stood on large tables between the sofa and chairs. Windows flanked each side of the fireplace. Outside the windows, the screened-in porch deck stretched around the fireplace side of the cabin.

The TV and DVD player sat on a weathered wooden desk with a storage area below. Inside were DVD movies. More DVDs were on the library shelves among the books. Porter shuffled through the DVD stacks and decided to put on "The Client." He grabbed the half-full bag of potato chips from the cupboard. He sat in one of the leather reclining chairs and leaned back. Within a few minutes, he had figured out how to operate the remote control for the TV and DVD player. He downed the rest of the chips and the can of Sprite. In the movie, the main character, an eleven-year old, was offered a can of Sprite in the hospital by a devious cop so the boy's fingerprints could be lifted from the can. The cop was sure the story he was getting from the boy was not the truth. "Your story is full of holes."

The movie was actually very good, not what Porter had suspected. He arose from the recliner and walked over to the books on the shelves. Some of the books had Mr. Downing's name as the author. Other books were by unknown authors to Porter. Some books and paperbacks were old and tattered. Some had new book covers. Porter actually liked to read. In junior high school, he regularly checked out sports-story books. He usually read one per night. His friends never read books because "it was a waste of time." He even kept his reading habit hidden from both his mother and dad. Porter never used the information he learned. His clusters of friends were "outcasts" as opposed to the "jocks" crowd. In fact even "geeks" treated Porter and his friends as "society outcasts."

Porter didn't care. His mother never understood him and didn't even like him. No matter what Porter did, she never took any time with him. She was always yelling at him.

Porter's dad never stood up to her. Until lately, Porter's dad was always quiet, never offering up any kind of opinion. While growing up, Porter was left to himself. Porter found solace in other friends who had family problems of all kinds, from drinking to drugs, to getting into trouble. Most of his friends came from divorced families where the mother worked to make ends meet.

Porter's real troubles started early in the seventh grade. Porter began shoplifting from different stores. Porter's friends showed Porter how to make a diversion so the key person could grab merchandise and hurry out the door. Sometimes the alarm would go off and a chase would ensue. These were the fun times for Porter. All kinds of department stores were targets for the shoplifting. Grocery stores were the best because they were busy and they didn't have alarms that went off. Also you could quickly consume the evidence. The only thing you had to watch out for were the one-way mirrors above the aisles. Usually, if the grocery store caught you, they tried to scare you and let you go with the promise that you wouldn't shoplift again. The grocery stores hardly ever called the police.

One day, Porter and his friend, Samuel, had each stolen some cigarettes. This time, however the assistant manager called the police. "We have a couple of shoplifters here."

Porter and Samuel were waiting in the manager's office upstairs, located above the checkout operations. The assistant manager questioned the boys sternly. "What grade are you guys in?"

"Tenth," replied Samuel.

"You ever shoplifted before?"

"Yeah, lots of times," replied Samuel.

"What happened when you got caught?"

"They always talked to us and warned us, but then they let us go and told us never to do it again."

Porter looked up towards the entrance on the far side of the store. "Oh, Oh! Look! It's your dad." The assistant manager overheard the comment.

Into the store, strolled the policeman. He walked up the stairs to the manager's office. The policeman looked at the two boys, one of them being his son. He was quiet for a few moments and then calmly said, "OK. I'll take them both down to the police station." He never said a word to his son. Porter knew they were both in deep trouble, especially Samuel. As the two boys and policeman were leaving the manager's office, Porter overheard the assistant manager talking to the manager, "Every shoplifter I've caught the last few times has always been caught before and then turned loose."

The manager replied, 'OK, from now on, just call the police every time. Let them take care of it."

The policeman escorted the two high school boys out of the store to the police cruiser.

That time was the first time Porter had been taken to the police station. Then he had to go to court. He was fined $150.00 and given a stiff warning. Porter had no job and no money. His parents paid the fine. From that time on, Porter's life turned into more misery, especially with his yelling mother, who now started despising Porter even more.

In junior high school, Porter had shoplifted often and got away with it. Sometimes, he got caught, but just like the assistant manager at Safeway said, they always let the shoplifters go when they promised to not do it again. Often, they would threaten to call the parents, but they usually never did. Both in junior high and senior high, Porter barely passed his school courses. In junior high, he copied and cheated on tests. Sometimes he and his friends would accost some younger student and even steal his homework before copying it. Porter and his friends ended up in the principal's office more and more. One time the principal caught Porter and two friends smoking in the bathroom. Porter's mother became a frequent visitor to the school. Each time she became angrier with Porter. Porter's one refuge at home was to sit in his bedroom late at night and read a sports book that he checked out of the library.

As a sophomore in high school, Porter had also begun cheating on tests. He mouthed off occasionally to teachers. Mostly he refused to turn in homework. He got caught smoking several times on both the school grounds and in the restrooms. Other than his friends from junior high, Porter had developed no new friends. Porter learned how to cuss. He lied often, to keep from getting caught at whatever mischief developed. He began withdrawing into himself. He was not a pleasant personality. His anger was always seething underneath. Porter shook his head and his whole body. "Where are these thoughts coming from?"

He chose another DVD, "Twister." As the movie concluded, Porter heard Mr. Downing coming through the screen door and onto the porch.

"Well, Porter, what do you want to have for supper? Do you want to go out for breakfast tomorrow?"

# Chapter 9

Ryan had awakened at 4:00 this morning. Starting again, on his new book, he had been typing and composing for about two hours. He guessed it was about 6:00 or 6:30. Yep, the clock on his computer showed "6:18." He went into the bathroom and showered, shaved, and combed his gray straggly hair. He was almost bald on top. Over his ears, white clumps of hair covered the sides of his head. Between haircuts, his whitish sideburns seemed to creep downward all of the time. He combed his hair straight back. The bristle hair on his neck grew profusely. "Guess I need to get a haircut next time I'm in town, before I see Kay. She is always reminding me to, '...look nice and dress nice.'" Kay was Ryan's daughter. They got together for lunch once a week, a routine he initiated after his divorce happened over twenty years ago.

The morning sun was just beginning to illuminate the emerging dawn. Birds were already gathering and chirping. "Well, I had better get Porter to wake up so we can go to breakfast." He went into Porter's bedroom and turned on the light. "Time to get up, Porter. Rise and shine." Porter grunted, turned over, and then remained motionless."

Ryan went into the living room and chose a classical orchestra CD. He turned the volume way up and the orchestra music cascaded over the whole cabin and sprawled into the two bedrooms. He went back into Porter's room. "Time to get up. Time to get up. Let's go to breakfast!" Ryan returned to the living room and started reading his Guideposts magazine. After reading several of the stories, he heard Porter stirring. Soon he heard the shower running. "That's amazing! Porter got up!"

Porter entered the living room. "What time is it?"

"Breakfast time!" answered Ryan.

Old man and young man went out to Ryan's Jeep. The morning coolness was slightly chilling... but invigorating. The morning sun beamed warmly. Ryan climbed into the driver's seat. Porter went around and started to climb into the passenger seat.

"Nope, Porter, back seat for you."

"You have got to be kidding!" Anger was rising inside Porter.

"You know the rules, Porter. When you are riding in a vehicle, you have to sit in the back seat. This is one of Judge Brown's rules. Sorry." Ryan smiled.

"What difference does it make?" said Porter demandingly.

"Evidently, Judge Brown has a reason or she wouldn't have put that stipulation into the rules. Climb in. I don't know about you but I'm hungry for some breakfast."

Porter climbed into the back seat on the passenger side and slammed the door.

"Got your seat belt on?"

78

As the two travelers started down the old logging road, five deer crossed in front of the Jeep. Ryan halted the Jeep and watched as the five brown furs blended into the pine tree forest. To the left side of the Jeep, a woodchuck sat on top of a rock and barked as the two Jeep travelers bounced by. Porter sat solemnly with his arms folded across his chest. Ryan guided the Jeep onto the highway and proceeded down the highway four miles to the Mountain Greenery Resort. Early in the morning, very few cars traversed this part of the highway. When they arrived at the restaurant, there were 3 SUVs and 4 pickups already there. Ryan and Porter entered through the screen door. Above the screen door, the bell tinkled. The hubbubs of conversation stalled a little as the old man and teenager walked in. They seated themselves in a booth by one of the windows.

"Hi Ryan, what have you been up to? Been getting any fishing in?"

"Hi, Jake. Hi Max, I hear you guys have been catching all the fish. You never leave any for the rest of us."

"Who's your friend here?"

"This is Porter. He's my summer guest."

The table conversations resumed. Most of the conversations were about weather, hunting, fishing, and aches and pains. Some stories Ryan had heard before, each time with the storyteller embellishing a little more. He was also always amazed at how much the old men enjoyed talking about machinery that had broken down and describing in detail how they got it to work again. Costs of everything were always going up. Some conversations revolved around the government and politics. Ryan always tried not to participate in these type conversations. Fishing stories and animal sightings were Ryan's interests. "Now, Porter, I know you said that you wanted to pay for your own breakfasts, but I'm now offering again to buy your breakfast."

"I can pay for my own!" snapped Porter.

Paulette strolled up to the table with the coffee pot and two menus in her hand. "Hello, Mr. Downing. Want some coffee?"

"Yes, and a glass of ice water, too. Paulette, this is Porter. Porter, this is Paulette. He's my guest for the summer."

"Welcome to the canyon. And what about you, Porter? Want something to drink?" Ryan particularly observed how well Paulette could remember names of people she just met.

"Orange juice," replied Porter.

"Small or large?

"Large."

"I'll be right back to take your order."

Paulette returned to the kitchen counter and grabbed two pots of coffee, one regular, and one Decaf. She deftly circled the room and refilled all the coffee cups for all the restaurant guests. She conversed with each table. Sometimes she sat down briefly at the individual booths. Everybody in the restaurant was friendly. Comings and goings were met with cheerful word exchanges. Laughter filled that little breakfast place. That was another one of the special reasons he enjoyed this cozy little conversation restaurant. Ryan read the saying written on the blackboard above the kitchen wall. Today's blurb was, "Go at life with abandon; give it all you've got. And life will give all it has to you."

Porter sat glumly, immersed into the menu. It appeared to Ryan that Porter was not accustomed to ordering from a menu. Paulette returned with coffee, water and orange juice. "You guys ready to order?" Do you want the 'Farmers Son,' Mr. Downing? Scrambled eggs?"

"Yes, with bacon and French toast. Porter, here, wants a separate check."

"And what would you like to order, Porter?" Porter looked up, surprised that someone already knew his name.

"I'll have the three egg Denver omelet, toast, side order of hash browns, side order of pancakes, and some biscuits and gravy ... and bacon."

"What kind of toast? White, wheat, sourdough, raisin?"

"Wheat toast."

"OK. I will put your order in."

Old man and teenager sat in silence. Ryan spoke up. "What kind of hobbies do you have that you like to do, Porter?"

"I don't have any hobbies."

"Well, what do you do in your spare time, when you are not going to school?"

"I'm spending my spare time here... with you in Colorado... as punishment," replied Porter in a bitter and sarcastic tone.

"Why do you feel you are being punished?"

"I didn't have a choice. I was ordered to be here!"

"Most folks would argue that a trip to stay in the mountains for a couple of months would be a marvelous vacation getaway."

"There's nothing to do here. It's boring."

"Well, we are out having breakfast together this morning in a restaurant full of happy friendly people. Outside the window there are majestic mountains. Even hummingbirds are showing up outside these windows. Can't you hear the river rushing by in the distance, over there?" said Ryan, pointing towards the open patio door. "There's more to do than you probably think, Porter. You just aren't peaceful yet."

"You are right about that!"

"Here's your breakfast, gentlemen. Enjoy!"

Porter was amazed at how dexterously Paulette carried the huge breakfast order on her two arms without dropping a plate. Paulette was a stocky girl with broad shoulders and a round face. Her eyes had a blue twinkle, a kind of hummingbird look, and heavy bushy brown eyebrows. When she smiled, which was most of the time, she exuded confidence and assurance. She seemed happy in her work. Ryan looked at Porter, "Would you like to pray for our breakfast, Porter?

"Pray?" said Porter.

"That's OK. I'll say the prayer. Lord, thank you for this breakfast and for the time Porter and I are together here in your majestic mountains. Guide our conversations and teach us in the way you would have us go. Thank you. Amen." Old man and young man ate in silence amidst the noisy semi-muffled conversations occurring throughout the restaurant.

"More coffee, Ryan?"

"Yes, thank you."

Paulette sat down next to Ryan, coffee pot in hand. "Porter, how long will you be staying up here?" Porter was surprised at the question and he hesitated before he responded.

"Well, uh... uh... until the middle of August, I guess."

"Would you like to get together with my friends and me tonight and play music? My roommate, Diane, and I get together with Sherry and Jeff up at our church for youth group. Then we are going over to Sean's house to play music. Sean is the youth group leader. Would you like to go?"

Startled, Porter replied angrily, "Church? Why would I ever want to go to a church?"

Unabashedly, Paulette retorted back, "My job is to invite you. You don't have to come. That's up to you."

Stammering, Porter was uncomfortable with this new encounter. He managed to get out, "I don't have a driver's license. I don't have a car."

"I have a car. I'm driving tonight. Five of us can fit in. We could pick you up on the way. Would that be all right with you, Mr. Downing? We really have a good time."

Ryan looked at the surprised boy sitting across the booth, "Sure, if that's what Porter wants to do."

Paulette stood up, "Do you want to go or not?"

Porter paused, "uh... uh... sure, OK."

"Where is the turnoff to your cabin, Mr. Downing?"

"Exactly 4.5 miles from here... on the left. There are two huge boulders with a fence gate between. My cabin is about a half mile off the main road. The mailbox has my name on it. I'll leave the gate open."

"Great, that's right on the way to the church. We will pick you up around 5:15, Porter. OK?"

Porter mumbled almost inaudibly, "I guess. OK."

Paulette returned to the other guests and continued the friendly chatter.

"Well, Porter, it looks like your prayer got answered. Now you have something to do today."

"I didn't pray," growled Porter.

Paulette brought the checks to the table. Ryan noticed that Porter's breakfast check was three times the amount of Ryan's. He pondered, "I must have a mighty hungry teenager on my hands who doesn't understand the value of money. I would rather go out to eat three different times than to blow it all on one meal."

"Would you like me to top off your coffee, Mr. Downing?"

"About half. Thanks."

"How about you, Porter. Can I get you anything else?"

"No."

"My roommate, Diane, is coming up and having lunch here with me on my lunch break at 11:00. She's going with us to youth group. If you are around at lunchtime, I can introduce you. We could all three have lunch together. I only have thirty minutes lunch because the noon rush starts around 11:30. What do you think?" It was a bold question Porter was not in any way expecting. Ryan looked at the befuddled teenager.

"Tell you what, Porter, we could go back to the cabin and get the fishing gear and head back here to fish that stretch of water there behind the restaurant. I can fish while you have lunch. We really don't have much of anything else planned for today."

Porter shrugged his shoulders, "Well, uh... OK, I guess..."

"We will eat out on the patio. See you then." Paulette stood up and started table-hopping again with the two coffee pots in hand.

He and Porter paid their individual tickets. Sharon took their money. Ryan used a debit card and added a tip. Porter gave Sharon a twenty-dollar bill. Porter took the change and placed a $2.00 tip on the table.

"Thanks for coming in, guys," smiled Sharon. "We will see you next time."

He opened the Jeep door and slid in. Porter went around to the passenger side and placed his hand on the passenger seat door handle. He stopped, as if pondering, and then climbed into the back seat."

Ryan smiled silently to himself. "Seat belt on?"

# Chapter 10

Ryan and Porter traveled silently until they arrived at the turnoff to the cabin. "What time is it?" asked Porter.

"I don't know. Why does it matter?"

"Just wondering..."

"Do you want me to bring along some fishing gear for you?"

"No," said Porter with a guttural sound.

The high rising sun was now glinting radiantly with yellow forest splendor. Ryan lowered the automatic windows. The Jeep engine emitted a soft reverberating echo into the warming velvety wind. Soon, they arrived back at the cabin. Porter sat in one of the rocking chairs on the porch while Ryan gathered up his fishing gear and his fishing vest. Ryan took along an apple and two raisin granola bars and placed his "Bluegrass Gospel Jam" baseball cap on his head. Porter sat in silence, his baseball cap now turned sidewise.

"Better put your hat on straight, Porter." Porter shrugged and pulled the brim to the front. "You might want to take along a book to read since you aren't fishing."

Porter went into his bedroom and selected from his suitcase one of the two sports story paperback books he had brought from Florida. Like chauffeur and rich boy, they returned to the restaurant parking lot. "There are some picnic tables where you can sit, Porter. There is a glider swing and some other tables closer to the stream. That's where I often do my reading. I'll be working my way upstream. You can have your lunch meeting while I fish."

"What time is it?" asked Porter.

"I don't know... probably about 10:00. Why does it matter? Well, I'm going fishing. River looks pretty full... probably have to fish from the riverbank a lot. See you later." Ryan strolled past the stream side of the restaurant and proceeded down to the open stretch of water. Porter trailed behind and remained at one of the picnic tables in the open grassy picnic and park area.

From this vantage point, Porter could see the back patio of the restaurant. He sat quietly for about ten minutes, pondering. Rambling thoughts spiraled through his mind. The sun's warm radiance gathered momentum. The sun arched hot upon Porter's skin. Flies found the perspiration pores on his arms. Porter soon sought out some soothing shade under the tall aspen trees that lined the riverbank. He sat on a shaded flat rock by the stream. He brought out the book he brought along and began reading. Porter still had full view of the restaurant patio. As he read, Porter became unconsciously aware of the sound of the rushing river coursing down the canyon. Upstream, around the bend, Mr. Downing disappeared.

Ryan found new river swirls behind submerged rocks, guarded by bushes that were usually on dry banks. He fished about an hour before the first fish strike. The rainbow trout leaped and was instantly gone. Fueled by the internal glee of almost catching a fish, the old fisherman crouched and climbed from pool to swirling pool. It was hard to fish this raging torrent. It was hard to guide his fly into the pools. "No matter. This is what fishing is all about."

He fished for another hour with no more strikes. He sat down in the shade on the bank and snacked on the granola bar and apple. "I wonder how Porter is getting along?"

Porter's reading was suddenly interrupted. Paulette was waving from the patio. "Hey, Porter! Come on up here!" Someone else was standing beside her. Porter tucked away his book in his back pocket, straightened his cap, and ambled slowly back to the patio area.

"This is my friend, Diane, my roommate... Diane, this is Porter. Here, sit down." Diane was a slender-frame girl, about the same height and age as Paulette, with short brown hair and friendly hazel eyes.

"I already know what Diane and I want for lunch." said Paulette, "What do you want? I'll put in your order for you."

"Bring me a hamburger and fries... and a coke."

"OK. I'll be right back." Paulette quickly vanished into the restaurant.

Diane spoke first, "I hear you are going with us to church youth group tonight."

"I guess." Porter was not accustomed to talking to people, especially friendly people, especially girls.

"That's good. We have a lot of fun."

"Church?" thought Porter, "Youth group?" "Fun?" Porter's mind was now becoming clogged with doubts and apprehensions. Paulette popped back onto the patio and sat down at the wrought iron table.

"Are you from around here?" asked Diane.

"Tampa, Florida," replied Porter.

"Are you moving here in the area?" Porter stalled, not really knowing what to say...exactly.

"He's staying at Mr. Downing's cabin for the summer," interjected Paulette. "... until the middle of August, right?"

"Oh the author," replied Diane. I haven't met him yet. I hear he writes Christian books."

Paulette continued. "Diane stays with me when she's not working in Fort Collins. She's a waitress for Village Inn there. She usually works the early morning shift. We worked it around so we have similar work schedules. She lives with her parents in Fort Collins five days a week and then spends her days off with me. She's saving up to go to a vocational training school to become a sports therapist. We both graduated from Fort Collins High School this past year. Our parents know each other. I'm saving up to go to an Architectural School to become an architect. My rent is free. It comes with my job."

"What grade are you in, Porter?" asked Diane.

"Well...uh...tenth grade, this year," Porter answered hesitatingly.

"Oh, you will get along well with Jeff," replied Diane. He will be in the eleventh grade. Jeff is coming tonight. Sherry is in eleventh grade, too. We all get along very well. Jeff will be happy we have another guy along. We girls outnumber the boys in our group. Jeff doesn't have much of a chance to get a word in edgewise." Porter's hamburger and the two girls' orders arrived simultaneously, delivered by Sharon. "Enjoy!"

The two girls bowed their heads. Paulette said a brief, prayer, much like Ryan's prayer this morning. Porter wondered what he was getting himself into. The friendly lunch was over in a jiffy. Paulette returned the dishes to the kitchen and resumed working with the noon rush guests. Diane stood up. "We will see you tonight, Porter. I hear we are picking you up."

"Yeah, I don't have a license or a car."

"OK, see you tonight." Diane left. She waved to Paulette as she passed through the screen door.

"See you later today, Polly."

"Want another coke, Porter?" asked Sharon, interrupting Porter's pensive thoughts.

"Sure."

Porter retrieved his book from his back pocket. The sun on the patio was hot, but Porter liked the warmth. The aspen trees surrounding the patio provided refreshing shade as the sun crept down the horizon. The searing sun reminded Porter of the Florida weather back home. The heat wasn't sweltering like it was back in Florida. This was more of a dry heat. He wanted to have a cigarette.

About an hour and a half later, Ryan strolled across the grassy picnic area.

"Have a good lunch?"

"Yeah."

# Chapter 11

Ryan leaned his fly fishing pole in the corner of the porch and placed his fishing vest on the floor beside the pole. In the shade of the cabin porch, man and boy sat in silent acceptance again. The wind picked up swirls of dust and slid through the pine trees. Surprisingly, Porter spoke up. "Did you catch any fish?"

"Two. Want to see them?" Ryan pulled out the small digital camera from the vest pocket of his crumpled fishing vest. He walked over to Porter's side and turned on the camera and scrolled past the last two images. Each picture showed a fish beside a fishing pole with a fly hooked in the trout's upper lip.

"Are you going to cook them?"

"No. I'm a catch and release fisherman. I have to hurry when I take the pictures so I can get the fish back in the water as soon as possible. It's usually better if I have someone along to help me. Usually, with the water up so high, the fishing isn't too much good, but today, I did all right. I caught them on an Adams Parachute Fly."

"You caught those fish with a fake fly?"

"Yeah, see... it's an Adams Parachute fly." Ryan gripped the fly in between his fingers. "The other flies I tried didn't work."

Porter paused for a moment, "Do you make your own flies? Is that feather and yarn stuff on the table inside for making flies?"

"Well, I actually buy most of my own flies. I don't have much patience for tying flies. My friend, Nathan comes up and he ties most of his own. He was the one who bought me the fly tying bench and vise. He brought everything up here for me to use. I'd rather fish with a fly that Nathan tied... than to spend time tying my own. Have you ever tied a fly, Porter? Would you like to learn?"

"No, I can't do that. I have never even thought about tying a fly."

Ryan noticed that Porter only answered his first question.

"Nathan is coming up to fish on Tuesday next week. Maybe he can show you a few things. When he was in high school, he started a fly-fishing business. At one time, he had four housewives tying flies for him. He supplied and sold the flies wholesale to local fishing stores and bait shops. He is a good fly fisherman. Nathan knows his flies. What time is the group picking you up today?"

Porter replied in a muttering tone, "5:15." In his mind he was thinking somberly, "I don't want to go to a church!"

"While I take a shower, how about you fix us some bacon, lettuce, and tomato sandwiches for supper?"

"I don't know how."

"I will tell you. Take that package of bacon out of the refrigerator and place the bacon strips side by side in the electric skillet. Put the heat dial on 350 degrees. Put the lid on...so the bacon doesn't pop on you or onto the cabinet. Just let the bacon sizzle until the strips start turning brown. Then use a fork to turn the strips over and brown them on the other side. When they look like they are done, put the bacon strips on a paper towel so the strips can drain and become crisp. Slice up a couple of those tomatoes and salt them. On that potato bread, put on some lettuce and mayonnaise. Then just put everything together. Cut the sandwiches in half and you are done. I'll be out of the shower by then."

Porter slowly followed instructions. He placed the sliced sandwiches on a paper plate and added some potato chips. He thought, "At least I won't have to wash as many dishes." His slicing of the tomatoes was irregular. He placed the thick and thin salted sliced red tomatoes alongside. He put a can of Sprite by his plate. "What do you want to drink?"

Ryan walked into the kitchen. "I'll have some milk."

Porter devoured the remaining bacon strips and salted tomatoes on a second sandwich. As promised, Mr. Downing let Porter wash the few dishes and clean up the kitchen, including the electric skillet. "What do I do with the grease in the skillet?" asked Porter.

"There's an empty can in the trash. Pour the grease in the can and take the trash out to the trashcan outside. Make sure you put the lid on tight. Keep that big rock on top. We don't want any bears stopping by."

"Bears?"

"Yes, Sharon, down at Mountain Greenery, said there was a black bear the other morning down by their trashcans. Critters of all kinds show up for human food leftovers. No need for us to encourage them. Don't worry. Bear sightings are very rare up around here. But they do show up once in a while."

"Have you ever seen a bear up here?"

"No, not around here. I saw a bear once, over on the other side of this canyon, coming up to Chambers Lake. It was a brown bear. He just came loping out of the woods and crossed in front of my Jeep. It was just a brief moment in time. I saw a mountain lion, once, in Wyoming, right around dusk. I saw a bobcat, here, at the cabin, down by the road, towards evening. He was pretty good-sized for a bobcat. Once in a while, I see a red fox. I've found that when you are alert to your surroundings, you begin noticing animals that you never knew were there. That's what happens when you slow down enough to observe. That's what cabin living is all about, slowing down... listening...appreciating... I think I hear a car coming. Go ahead. I'll finish the cleanup in the kitchen. You can go meet your new friends. I'll be there in a minute."

Porter walked off the porch and down the steps. A gray flaking-paint noisy Jeep popped into the clearing. Paulette was driving. In the passenger seat was Diane. In the back seat were another girl and a boy. Paulette turned off the ignition. Paulette and Diane hopped out of the Jeep. The two passengers in the back seat climbed out, too. Ryan walked down the steps. Paulette seemed to be in charge. She began the introductions.

"Hi Porter, Mr. Downing... these are my friends, Sherry, Jeff, and Diane. Guys, this is Mr. Downing and Porter."

Jeff shook hands with Porter and Ryan. "Nice to meet you." Porter was quiet.

"You have a nice cabin here, Mr. Downing," said Jeff.

"Thanks."

Paulette spoke up. "Well, let's get going. Everybody climb back in."

Diane got in the back seat with Sherry and Jeff, leaving the front passenger seat open for Porter. Porter hesitated. Ryan stepped up. "I know it sounds strange to you all, but Porter needs to ride in the back seat. He's not allowed to ride in the front seat."

"OK," said Diane, puzzled, as she climbed back into the passenger seat in front. "How come?"

"Restrictions," replied Mr. Downing, "... and on the way back, too. Thanks, guys." Mr. Downing waved as the Jeep proceeded out of the clearing and back to the highway.

Back on the highway, the atmosphere in the Jeep was subdued. Paulette spoke up, "What did he mean by 'restrictions?'"

Porter hesitated briefly then calmly replied, "When I'm riding in a vehicle, I'm required to sit in the back seat..." He offered no further explanation. As the five teenagers traveled up the canyon, lively talk and chatter resumed. Porter remained quiet, befuddled by his brand new people surroundings. After about fifteen minutes driving, Paulette guided the Jeep into the graveled church parking lot. A wooden weathered sign displayed, "Chapel in the Pines." The church building was made out of flagstone. Over the entrance door in front was a steeple with a white wooden cross, mounted on top. The church was appropriately named because it was nestled among the pine trees. In the back of the church, just a short way in the distance, the river curved and flowed by. This was a very serene and peaceful setting. Even Porter was somehow aware of some unfamiliar peaceful feeling.

The group piled out of the Jeep. They grabbed their musical instruments that were stacked in the trunk area behind the back seat. Porter noticed that each teenager in the group carried a Bible. Porter again wondered, "What's this all about? What am I getting myself into?"

To the left side of the church, inside the "Fellowship Room," they called it, behind the sliding folding door, was another ample sized room full of folding chairs placed in a large semi-circle. Paulette introduced Porter to Sean. "Hi, Porter, I'm Sean, the youth pastor here at the church. Come on in and make yourself comfortable. Welcome."

A couple of other teens had already gathered in the room. Soon the conversations were spirited and noisy. The four Jeep passengers brought out their instruments and began tuning them. It reminded Porter of the one time in junior high school, when the music teacher took the whole class to a concert in a huge auditorium. It seemed like the whole orchestra was discordantly tuning at the same time. That's when Porter first heard the "1812 Overture by Tchaikovsky." Strangely enough, he had really enjoyed the whole concert.

Sean spoke up, announcing to everyone. "This is Porter. It's his first time here. Our format, Porter, on Wednesday nights is to request that everyone share a bible verse that has helped him or her during the past week or month, sometimes as recently as the day before. You don't have to worry about a bible verse tonight. It's all a volunteer event. Afterwards, we have some fun with bluegrass gospel music. My wife, Kristin, has some pumpkin bars baking in the kitchen, along with some hot apple cider. She will be in soon to sing along with us."

"OK," said Sean, "who has a bible verse to share?'

Diane spoke up right away. She had her bible tabbed with a yellow sheet of paper. "I do. In Second Corinthians, Chapter 5, Verse 7... It says, 'We live by faith, not by sight.'

The cashier, Sarah, where I work at Village Inn, just recently had her infant son die. He was only about two months old. She has another older son about three years old. Right now, Sarah is up in Montana staying with her folks. Sarah's husband is not a believer. She told me one time early on that her husband was angry with God. With the new baby dying, I don't know how this situation will turn out. We need to pray that God will help them in this time of grief and probably, despair."

There was a silent pause.

Jeff spoke up next, "Cast all your anxieties on him because he cares for you... First Peter 5... 7." Jeff offered no further expository.

Paulette had her bible open. Underlined was the verse, James 5, Verse 13. She read aloud, "Is any one of you in trouble? He should pray. Is anyone happy, let him sing songs of praise. That's why I like music. Singing helps with life's loads. I read that statement once in a Guidepost magazine."

Sean smiled, bowed his head, and said, "Lord, please help us with these requests and situations. Bless each one of these young people here. Amen. On that note, let's play some music."

Sean picked up his guitar from the stand in the corner. Paulette finished tuning her guitar. Jeff had an instrument that looked like the curly instrument Porter had seen in Mr. Downing's cabin. Sherry had a banjo. Diane started drawing a hairy bow across the violin strings. One of the other teenagers in the group was playing a stand-up base that he had retrieved from another room.

"Let's do, 'I'll Fly Away,'" announced Sean. Sean was a finger picker with a Chet Atkins style triple-picking harmony. Sean's guitar was a twelve-string Taylor guitar. "Do you want to take a mandolin break, Jeff? Kick it off, Sherry..."

The banjo rumbled resoundingly and the song soared high in that little church room. Porter sat back, amazed at the precision and huge volume of music booming from those few musicians. Each of the musicians seemed to know all of the words of the song. Porter did not recognize any of the songs. Every so often, Sean would call out, "Fiddle" or "Mandolin." The group would back off and the featured musician would continue and play an instrumental break. As the song regained momentum, Porter immediately found himself enjoying this strange new style music. It was fast and unique. Porter was amazed at the skill these young musicians possessed.

"Who has the next song?" asked Sean.

Diane announced, "How about, 'On the Wings of a Dove, in 'D'?"

"OK. Kick it off with the fiddle, Diane." Porter recognized this song from somewhere back in his memory. The tune sounded familiar to him. This song was slower and at a different rhythm. The teens sang along with this tune, too...everyone was having a good time... even Porter. Kristin came in from the kitchen and joined in amidst the musicians.

Sean was the leader of the musical group. He let each musician take a turn in the selection of songs. The other teen in the room was even asked to choose a song. Porter was amazed that everyone knew all the songs, even all the words. "How about you, Porter? Do you have a song you would like for us to play?"

"I don't know any songs."

"OK. You can pass, for now. Sherry, how about doing, 'Unclouded Day' in G? Go for it, Sherry!"

Sherry and the banjo came alive with a rapid thumping beat. The other musicians joined in and each musician took an instrumental break. Kristin sang into the microphone that Sean had set up earlier. Porter was soon enveloped in the musical ambiance. He was actually enjoying being drawn into the music... and the group. Even if it was for a few brief minutes, Porter's residing anger and sullen disposition started melting away. He wasn't thinking at all about being in a church. The singing and playing musicians kept up their non-stop playing for about 45 minutes.

Kristin announced, "We have warm pumpkin bars and hot apple cider in the kitchen!" All the teens gathered in the kitchen. Paulette asked Sean how to finger a particular chord position that Sean had used during one of the songs.

Porter gathered his dessert and apple cider and sat with the group. Conversation revolved around mountain topics, to meetings and happenings in the canyon. Paulette and Diane were avid about fishing. Jeff, the mandolin player, enjoyed horseback riding. Sean and Kristin, the leaders, often set up music gigs at various restaurants and RV parks so they could share music whenever and wherever possible. Each event was welcome to any teen musician who wanted to come along. "It's our outreach," said Sean.

Sitting next to Porter, Jeff spoke up, "Yeah... that's how I got to coming here. Everyone came over and played at our bunkhouse, we call it. They let me join in with my mandolin on the very first time they came."

"Bunkhouse?" questioned Porter.

"Yeah... at the ranch where I am staying."

"You live on a ranch up here in the mountains?" asked Porter.

"No, I don't live up here. I'm just staying for the summer. It's a ranch for teenagers with problems. A judge placed me here against my wishes. It's actually a good place to get peaceful. I really enjoy riding and taking care of the horses. I had to get permission to come over here to this church. I really enjoy playing my mandolin."

"Let's go in and play our final wrap-up song before we leave," announced Sean.

Everyone in the group returned to the fellowship room. "'Will the Circle be Unbroken" in G,'" announced Sean.

Diane led off with her fiddle and played the chorus slowly one time through. Then the entire music group joined in at a high-speed beat. The rousing song again filled the fellowship room. Afterwards, everyone repacked the instruments into their cases. On the way out, Sean shook Porter's hand. "Nice to have you come, Porter, hope you can come again. You are always welcome."

"Thanks, ..." replied Porter thoughtfully, "maybe I can."

"Porter, this is a little bold of me, but somehow I feel like you have never been to a church before. Do you even own a Bible?"

Porter didn't know how to respond. Sean went over to the wall where some books were displayed. "Here, I'll give you a Bible. It's the 'Living Bible,' the one I used when I first started becoming a Christian. You can borrow it. It's in every-day English so it's easier to understand. You have to look over all the underlined verses. I kind of went overboard underlining verses. Thanks again for coming tonight."

Porter rejoined the group in Paulette's Jeep. He sat resolutely in the back seat. He placed the "newly-acquired" bible beside his feet on the floor. The other four teens were joking around and having a good time. Porter was silent. He was the first person to be dropped off. He was embarrassed holding the Bible in his hand. He kept it hidden as much as he could. Paulette turned her head towards the back seat and asked, "Coming to breakfast in the morning?"

"I don't know..."

"OK. See you later. Thanks for coming." The gray Jeep melded noisily into the forest darkness.

"Hi Porter, how did it go?"

"We had a lot of music."

Porter observed the open DVD case. Ryan was watching the movie, "The Apartment." It was strange...the movie was black and white. The fireplace across the room was glowing red. Porter thought for a few moments... and then headed towards his bedroom. "Are we going out to breakfast in the morning?"

# Chapter 12

As normal, Ryan was up early... at 4:00 AM. He felt encouraged to write. First, he responded to some emails that had come in last evening. He sent out his daily "Bible Verse Blurbs of Wisdom" to everyone on his Bluegrass Gospel Jam email roster. He had accumulated and assimilated all the Bible verses included in his books. He sent out one verse each day. Almost every week, Ryan received back comments, telling him how much the verses "... hit the spot. It's just what I needed...thank you."

He reviewed the first chapter he had just finished composing. Ryan edited his writings as he went along, changing and editing words and phrases. That way, to Ryan, his writing flowed more easily and was more focused. Even choosing a new word to use from the Thesaurus helped mold and expand his thoughts. He usually left the "whole-document spelling and grammar checking" as the last step before the book was ready to be published. He used an online "print on demand" Internet publisher to print his books. Ryan had a good grasp of English skills, punctuation, spelling, and continuity flow. He felt that God was definitely, and continually, guiding him with the words and ideas that surged onto paper. Two-finger typing was slow, but deliberate. He had never learned to type. He felt that his two-finger slow typing speed allowed him to orchestrate and coordinate his thoughts in a more lucid and clearer fashion.

He was becoming a more proficient writer with each completed new book. This current book was book number seven.

According to his computer clock at the bottom of the screen, it was 6:45 AM. Ryan had been writing for almost three hours. He heard Porter stirring. Ryan hustled into the bathroom, took a shower and shaved. When he emerged from the bathroom, Porter was sitting by the fireplace, sifting through the DVD movies.

"Find one you want to watch?"

"What's this 'Mr. Baseball' about?"

"It's a story about an American baseball player who gets traded to a baseball team in Japan. It's a good movie. I think there is enough hot water for your shower. I tried to hurry. We will head down to the restaurant as soon as you are ready."

Ryan went into the living room and looked out the window at the emerging daylight. The mornings were intensifying earlier and earlier each day. The wind had been fairly calm all this last week. "This would be a good day to fish up at the lake. Maybe Porter would like to go with me."

He started up the Jeep. The Jeep clock displayed 8:45. This time, Porter automatically climbed into the back seat. They headed down to Mountain Greenery. When they arrived, the restaurant was bubbling with activity. Ryan read the saying above the pass-through-window to the kitchen,

"Realize that you are greater than you've ever considered yourself to be."

Only one booth was not occupied. "Hi guys," said, Paulette, ushering them inside. "Take that last booth and I'll be with you in a few minutes. Coffee, water...orange juice?"

"Yes," replied Ryan.

"OK," said Porter.

Paulette headed back to the kitchen to pick up and serve a large order. There was a sizeable group of folks sitting at the center table area. To Ryan, it looked like one whole huge family of grandpas, grandmas, kids, and grandkids. Everyone seemed to be talking at the same time with five different conversations going on simultaneously. He gazed intently at the teen sitting across from him. He wondered what Porter was thinking about. "What thoughts are residing in Porter's mind? How do an old man and a young teenager find something in common to talk about?"

"So, how was the youth group?"

"Fine," replied Porter.

"What did you do?"

"Mostly music. Then we had pumpkin bars and apple cider."

"What kind of music, singing?"

"They called it 'bluegrass gospel' or 'gospel bluegrass' ... anyway it was something called bluegrass... We mostly sat in a circle and each person played a different instrument, except for about three of us. Jeff played a small curly instrument like the one up in your cabin. Another guy played a huge stand-up fiddle-looking instrument. Sean, the leader, played a twelve-string guitar. Actually, the playing sounded good. Everyone seemed to know all the songs… except me."

Ryan was amazed when so much information had unexpectedly emerged from Porter. Usually, Porter grumbled "one-word" or "one-short-sentence replies." Porter hardly ever expounded on responses.

"A curly instrument? You mean a mandolin?"

"I think that's what they called it. It made a high-pitched 'twangy' sound. They all took turns choosing the songs."

"Can I take your orders?" Paulette asked. "Do you want the same as yesterday?"

"Yes, I'll have my usual."

"Porter?"

"I'll have a large stack of pancakes, and a side order of bacon."

"Separate checks?"

"Yes," replied Ryan. "You sure are busy this morning…"

"Yes, it's a group who all came up for a family reunion and a wedding. They are also having a special wedding rehearsal dinner here tomorrow night. I'll be helping with the Friday night meal. The wedding is happening Saturday morning at the church. It will probably be extra busy for the normal Saturday noon rush. The family knows Vic and Sharon. The bride's parents used to come up here every summer and stay all summer. The bride said she used to work up here as a waitress, too. I'll put your order in, but it will probably take longer than normal... since it is so busy."

"That's OK. Porter and I are in no hurry. I could use some more coffee... when you get a chance."

"Sure."

Outside the window beside the booth, several hummingbirds hovered almost motionless and flittered in front of the red liquid in the feeders. It was as if the hummingbirds were curiously observing the human ongoing breakfasts inside the restaurant. One brightly colored bird hovered directly outside the window beside Porter. Porter studied the tiny hummingbird's activities a few inches away from his face. He put his finger on the windowpane. The sudden human movement caused the hummingbird to dash away. All of a sudden, the miniature bird returned with another strikingly colored hummingbird. To Porter, it looked like two helicopters were poised for landing on an aircraft carrier. Porter gulped his orange juice. Ryan also gazed at the delirious dance outside the window. He sipped his steaming coffee. "I'm hiking up to the lake today, Porter. Do you want to come along?"

"How far is it?"

"About a mile and a half. Takes a little over an hour. The fishing is usually good. The wind is blowing today, so that will make the fishing a little more challenging."

"I don't think so," grumbled Porter. "I don't like to fish... or hike."

Porter had now resumed his negative attitude demeanor, grunting out his sentences with a low angry guttural sound. Ryan briefly ignored Porter's attitude.

"I received an email from Nathan. He confirmed that he is planning on spending the day next Tuesday. He usually likes to fish the stream. He's a catch-and-release fisherman, too. If you want, he might show you some fly tying techniques." Porter sat solemnly with his arms crossed across his chest. He slouched even more while they waited on the breakfasts to arrive.

The noisy activity in the restaurant began diminishing as the whole reunion family headed out to do mountain activities. There were a lot of hugs and smiles passed around. Now, there were only a few restaurant guests. Paulette and Sharon began quickly carting the dishes into the kitchen, cleaning the tables as they went. Soon the interior tables were separated in the center. Sharon began cleaning the booth tables that had also been used. Paulette returned with a pot of coffee and a glass of ice water. She refilled Ryan's coffee cup. She sat down beside him, opposite Porter.

"Did you enjoy youth group last night, Porter?"

"Uh...uh... it was OK... I guess..." Porter remained in a squatty slouch.

"I saw Sean give you a Bible last night. Have you started reading it yet?"

"No... I don't believe in that Bible shit!"

Ryan winced as Porter spurted out the profanity, especially in front of a girl.

Unabashedly, Paulette spit back words to Porter, "Well... have you ever read the Bible, ever?"

"No, I don't need to."

"Then how can you say you don't believe something you have never read?" Paulette paused. "You must be a person full of huge faith to say you don't believe... if you don't even know what it says." Paulette stared directly at Porter, taking an adamant pose as if being a television interviewer. "Have you ever been to church, Porter?"

"No..."

"That's a lie, Porter. You just went to church last night. What do you call that? Didn't your family ever take you to church?"

Porter shifted uneasily in his seat. He offered no response to Paulette's boldness. He didn't know how to respond. Porter's internal protection system kicked in with more smoldering anger and quiet somberness. He rapidly retreated from the confrontation that was being forcefully advanced by Paulette's probing questions. Paulette stood up, coffee pot in hand. Ryan interrupted, "Porter said you and your friends played Bluegrass Gospel Music last night."

Paulette's eyes sparkled. "Yes," she smiled. "We get together every Wednesday night at church and play music. We do it all summer." Paulette's conversation was friendly and seemingly unabashed at the confrontation words she had just used with Porter. Paulette was simply a very perceptive individual, seemingly unaffected by reference to the word, "shit."

"Did you know," continued Ryan, "that I put on Bluegrass Gospel Jam events?"

"No, I didn't know," responded Paulette, "When and where? Can anyone come?"

"Well I don't have the Gospel Jams during the summers. I spend my summers up here writing and fishing. But, starting in September, we hold them in Fort Collins on the second Saturday of every month from 12:00 to 4:00. I have helped start up other Gospel Jams across the country, too. We have one in Florida, one in Massachusetts, and about seven others in Colorado. We offer free instrument workshops at the Fort Collins Jams."

"Sounds like a lot of fun."

"Yes. We do have a lot of fun. We take turns choosing the songs, and we include the audience, too. I have an idea, Paulette. How would you and your friends like to come up to my cabin and play some music some night? I already have instruments and some songbooks. You could bring your whole youth group. He gave a sidelong glance towards Porter. "I think it would be an enjoyable time. How about a week from this Saturday, at 6:00?"

Paulette's face beamed. "I'll see what everybody is doing. Could the youth pastor and his wife come too? They are the head organizers of our group."

"Absolutely. Invite as many as you want..." He's eyes again glanced over at the slouching teenager. "We will look forward to it."

When Porter and Ryan climbed into the Jeep, He turned and asked Porter in staccato fashion, "Are you always this grouchy, Porter? Do you practice your anger all the time? Don't you even know how to carry on a civil conversation? Can't you control your language? Don't you know you just embarrassed me? Can't you keep your cuss words to yourself? And by the way, you are not to use 'shit' any more, especially in front of people who are trying to be friendly with you. Be angry on your own time, not on mine!"

# Chapter 13

Upon returning to the cabin, neither Porter nor Ryan spoke. Ryan donned his fishing vest and prepared to go fishing. After putting on his hiking boots, he stopped at the porch screen door. "Are you sure you don't want to go fish the lake?"

Porter frowned a reply, "No..."

"While I'm gone, I'm going to give you a chore to do. Saturday, you and I are going to the grocery store in Fort Collins. I want you to make out a grocery list of what we need. In addition, I want you to plan out all the supper meals for every day of next week. Whatever we have to eat is whatever you buy... and cook."

"I don't know how to cook! I have told you that before! How many times do I have to tell you?"

"I don't care for your attitude, Porter. You don't even want to try! Well, it's not going to be very peaceful around here if you keep polishing that negative ego of yours. There are some cookbooks in the kitchen cabinet. Find some recipes you can prepare and make out your grocery list accordingly. I suggest you take a mental inventory of what we already have so we don't buy double. We are almost out of toilet paper. Have the list on the counter so I can review it when I get back."

"When are you coming back?"

"When I feel like it... after I calm down from having to deal with you. It's time you started meeting me half way, Porter. You can always leave this cabin earlier so you can get to jail sooner! The judge told me that you have some potential, Porter... use that head of yours and get off that stinking thinking pattern. This is a beautiful setting... don't spoil it!"

As Ryan stepped down from the porch, he told Porter, "Also, think of something to serve when the youth group comes up. And... start thinking how to become nice and congenial. If you don't know what 'congenial' means, look it up in the dictionary! I expect to see that grocery list on the counter when I get back!"

Ryan's temper began subsiding as he hiked up the trail towards the lake. The exercise and mountain serenity was the best therapy activity he had. The beauty lying around the mountains molded Ryan's thoughts, focused his thoughts, and even created new inspirational thoughts. "Lord, I really need some help here..."

Ryan rested several times on the path. He gazed upwards. In front of wispy white pillow clouds, a huge bird with a large wingspan circled high above. "Must be some sort of hawk." Forest squirrels and songbirds sent up their melodious prattle. Like invisible shadow ghosts, the restless wind currents began winding through the trees, scattering and relocating dry leaves.

He arrived at the lake. He removed his chair from its green nylon sleeve and unfolded it. He sat the chair beside a huge fifteen-foot boulder on the bank of the lake. This was one of his favorite fishing spots. The boulder offered cooling shade and also acted as a windbreak, depending on which way the wind decided to blow. He rigged his casting pole with a clear plastic bubble filled with water. The fly was tied about five feet back on the end of the line. From his metal fly box in his fishing vest, he selected a fly with yellow tufts. Soon he was tossing out the bubble with a "swish" and a "ploop!" He reeled in the fly slowly, deliberately and steadily.

"Aaah... this is what life is all about..." Ryan basked in the sun and shade. His thoughts turned towards heaven. Somehow he felt included, encompassed by a warm feeling, not the sun, but like an enveloping caress from the wind. When He returned to the cabin, about 5:30, he guessed, a scribbled grocery list lay on the counter. Beside the list were three different cookbooks with strips of paper as bookmarks. Porter was just finishing watching the movie, "Mrs. Doubtfire."

"What are we having for supper, Porter?"

"Hamburgers. I already started up the coals."

After supper, Porter and Ryan watched the movie, "Hoosiers," which Porter had chosen. After the movie, old man and teenager sat rocking on the porch. As the night crept in, the wind started circling and buffeting. It was a warm wind. "Feels like the weather is changing... probably a front coming in..." commented Ryan wistfully.

Later, after both cabin visitors tried to go to sleep, the wind started a roar and shook the windows and rattled and banged the cabin front door and the porch screen door. The trees outside swayed jerkily back and forth, bending and bowing to the bursting gusts. The wind started a high-pitch whining sound as it encircled the corners of the cabin. Some of the cold air sifted through the doors and windows. Both sleepers curled up deeper in the warmth of the plaid wool blankets. Ryan looked out his bedroom window. The moonlight spilled over the forest floor. Shadows danced and permeated the cabin surroundings. Ryan felt at peace. He enjoyed the weather, any kind of weather.

The teenager slept like a log.

# Chapter 14

The buffeting wind continued to howl at a ferocious roar until early morning. Ryan was up at 4:30. He didn't feel like writing, but he was already up, so he prodded himself to get started. As soon as he got into it, the words started flowing from his mind into his computer. He kept at his task until about 7:00. He fixed himself some granola cereal with a sliced banana as garnish. He downed the last of the orange juice. The wind had suddenly stopped. He decided to hike back up to the lake again. He looked in on the teenager. Porter was still soundly sleeping... "No need to wake him up. He doesn't want to go fishing, anyway."

Ryan fixed himself a ham and cheese sandwich to carry along. He added an apple and two granola bars and a small bottle of Artesian drinking water. He picked up a notebook from the kitchen counter and turned to a blank page. He wrote a note to Porter. "Porter, I've gone fishing up at the lake. I don't know exactly when I'll be back. You are welcome to hike up and join me. Just come on up. I think the fishing will be very good... Mr. Downing."

It was cool this morning from the cold front ushered in by last night's wind. He headed up the slim thread-like trail to the lake. The physical effort and exertion quickly warmed Ryan's body. He hadn't been up to the lake this early in the morning. The morning was afresh with pungent pine tree odors and newly dropped pinecones. The forest chatter came alive. He cherished these peaceful and solitude moments. He felt like a welcomed guest. He scrutinized the mountain glory and majesty all around him. As he steadily ambled up the trail, again, his thoughts turned towards God.

He pondered, "Why did I leave Porter all alone today? I'm sure he won't come up to fish with me. There's no telling what Porter will do with his time. He keeps driving me up the wall. I know I shouldn't worry about it, but I really don't know how to deal with him. What am I supposed to do, Lord?"

A young gray-furred white-cottontail rabbit scurried across the trail and stopped by a sun-dried straggle bush. Alongside the trail, two ground squirrels darted jerkily up and over the rocks. Ryan stopped and watched the activity. Three blue jays swooped down from a high pine branch and swiftly ascended to the next tree limb on the adjoining tree. The mountain forest was never really quiet. Still, the serenity encircled Ryan with a subdued effervescence. The forest had a tranquil symphony all its own. The multi-weather mountain cabin setting granted permission to Ryan to deliberately become a daily participant in the enveloping sounds and winds of the forest. For Ryan, the ambiance was an always-refreshing experience and offered the most enjoyable times. He believed that God spoke unobtrusively in a calm unseen, unheard, but mystical manner. Going fishing was only part of this omnipresent experience. Ryan's mind always cleared when he was a visitor within "God's playground," as he called his surroundings. A hike into this part of the wilderness provided new thoughts for his writings... as well as calm-down thoughts for dealing with an angry teenager. "I sure wish Porter would come up and experience this serenity."

Groggily, Porter sat up in bed. There was a quiet stillness in the cabin. The wind was now at rest even though Porter was unaware of the continual roaring last night. He went into the kitchen and read the note, "Gone Fishing." He fixed some Cheerios cereal for breakfast and ate an apple. He also peeled an orange. This time, he cleaned up the kitchen and put away the dishes. He showered and shaved and came back to the kitchen. "Well, what do I do today? I'm trapped here in this cabin." Porter went over to the CD player and played one of Mr. Downing's CDs. It was a rock and roll CD from the 50's. Not Porter's style, but the music was actually enjoyable...

Porter picked up the Fly Fishing book from the table where the fly tying materials lay. He sat down on the couch in front of the fireplace and began looking at the pictures and fly-tying diagrams. Before long, Porter was engrossed in the fascinating book. Porter did enjoy reading, but it was usually his sports stories that he silently read and kept hidden away from his mother and dad. Porter could assimilate information easily. He just didn't recognize any use for reading books. "How could anyone ever read all the books in a library, anyway?"

This book was different. It described not only how to tie a fly, but also how to fish with it, and the best times of the year to use it. It even described the techniques of casting with a fly pole. There were lots of result pictures, showing which fly was used to catch different trout species. The fish photos were just like the ones in the digital camera Ryan had shown him yesterday.

Porter was still somewhat bored. He walked over to the CD player. He chose and started playing another of Mr. Downing's CDs.

"Classical Treasures"

Strauss

"The Blue Danube"

As the waltz gathered momentum, Porter returned to the Fly Tying book. He became interested in one particular fly pattern. The book explained and displayed each step. Porter began following the instructions. In his younger days, he had always been good at putting model airplanes and cars together. Porter started sifting through the materials on the desk. Tying a fly didn't look all that difficult. A little clumsily at first, Porter began the process. He enjoyed each of the challenging steps. As "The Blue Danube" played in the background, Porter found himself doing something creative. He also felt the sensation of silence in his surroundings. He figured out how to use the vise attached to the fly-tying table. Abruptly, Porter was hungry. He stretched, stood up, and walked out to the porch. The weather was warming up fast. Porter went back into the kitchen and fixed two peanut butter and jelly sandwiches. This time, he included a glass of milk. He added some potato chips to his plate. He also found a jar of polish dill pickles. He placed two pickle spears on his plate. "Something different," he thought.

Most of the morning had passed by. He hadn't quite finished tying his first fly. He was having trouble pulling thread through the thread tool and wrapping around the shank of the hook. He put on another CD. "Rock & Roll Music from the 50's" boomed out. The teenager sat on the porch steps with his knee holding open the screen door. In the trees surrounding the clearing, in the distance, he noticed a slight brownish-colored movement. Soon, a buck deer meandered across to the other side of the clearing. His brown body was soon silhouetted into the trees. "Maybe he likes Rock and Roll."

Porter returned to his fly tying activity. For some unknown reason, he was challenged now to get something finished. Finally, he completed the last step, using some glue to hold some tiny flared feathers on top of the fly. As soon as the glue dried, he compared his artistic work to the final product picture. In no way, did the two resemble the same pattern. In short, Porter's fly was "ugly." To Porter, it didn't even look like any sort of insect. Even part of the upper wings had flaked off.

"I think I will watch a movie."

He selected, "The Shawshank Redemption," a movie about a man falsely sentenced to prison for killing his wife. He sipped on a can of Sprite as he sprawled on the couch in front of the fireplace. In one of the kitchen cabinets, he found a jar half-full of dry roasted salted peanuts. Soon the jar was empty. After watching the movie, Porter walked around the clearing in front of the cabin. After four successive round trips, he stopped by the thin trail that led up to the lake. "I wonder what time it is. I wonder where this trail goes."

Porter slowly wandered up the trail. He stopped and stood in the shade of the tall pine trees. As he continued following the gradually sloping trail, he turned around and surveyed the trail behind him. Behind him, the cabin had disappeared into the woods. He sat down on a white dry log that, many years ago, had fallen in the forest. At the other end of the log, at a rotting spot, bugs and ants scurried in and out. Flies circled and buzzed. Porter sat quietly while the "Blue Danube Waltz" melody returned and danced in his mind. Porter sat there. His mind disengaged. No thoughts were coming. He didn't know how long he had been sitting there. Suddenly, Porter was aware of something coming down the trail. Fear encompassed his whole body. His first thought startled him. "A Bear?"

"Hey, Porter, were you coming up to fish with me?" asked Ryan, coming into view.

Shaking internally, Porter replied, " No... I just took a walk..."

"Pretty up here, isn't it?"

Porter suppressed his anxiety. He instantly changed into being subdued in spirit, trying not to show any emotion.

"How about having spaghetti tonight? I make an exceptionally good spaghetti sauce! I'll show you how to make it."

Ryan pulled out the small camera from the pocket in his fishing vest. "Take a look at these pictures. These are two of the fish I caught. It's an awesome and beautiful day."

# Chapter 15

Last night, after the spaghetti supper, the two cabin visitors watched two movies, one right after the other. The first movie was, "The Edge," all about a billionaire and two work associates who survived a plane crash into a wilderness lake up in Canada. While they were lost, a huge bear tracked and chased them, even attacking and killing one of them. It was a definite compelling story about survival and betrayal. Porter remembered his brief unexpected shaking experience earlier that day on the trail.

The second movie was, "28 Days," about a woman who entered an alcohol and drug treatment center after she crashed a limousine into a house on her sister's wedding day. The movie displayed all her anger and non-acceptance of group therapy sessions.

"It was a very powerful treatise on what recovering drug and alcohol patients do in everyday life, before reality sets in," Porter thought. He was definitely moved in spirit by the movie presentation.

About halfway through the second movie, Ryan went to bed. In the morning, Ryan and Porter headed the Jeep out the clearing to the main road and proceeded to Mountain Greenery. For about twelve minutes, no conversation transpired between the two travelers.

"Did you bring the grocery list?" asked Ryan.

"I forgot."

"Guess you will have to shop from memory, then."

At the restaurant, a new quote was written on the white board.

"If all the birds in the forest waited until they were good enough to sing, then the chorus of the forest would never start. Do you have a song in your heart? Suggestion: Sing while you can, today. Tomorrow is always uncertain."

"Where did you find that saying, Paulette? I like that phrase, 'chorus of the forest.' Did you or Sharon come up with it?"

"Sharon let me choose what to post. I saw that one in a dentist office. Sometimes I write something myself. I write little thoughts here and there. I'm trying to find out how to write a song so I can play it on my guitar. I would like to sing my own song. I think that would be a wonderful achievement. By the way, I talked to everyone in our youth group, including Sean and Kristin. They all said they would come up for jamming at your cabin next Saturday. Everyone was excited about it. What can I get you guys for breakfast?"

Soon, the breakfasts arrived. Ryan bowed his head and said a silent prayer. Paulette returned with a pot of coffee. "What are you guys up to today? Fishing?"

"No, we have to go grocery shopping so we have food to eat next week. Maybe later this afternoon, we will go. I caught up a couple of good ones yesterday, and the day before, up at the lake.

"Diane and I love to go fishing. We go all summer long, when we are not working. We fish the river a lot."

"The river is flowing high right now... not too easy to fish with the early spring runoff," replied Ryan. "Why don't you and Diane come up and fish by my cabin sometime? You would be welcome any time you wish. You can either fish the stream or hike up to the lake."

"That would be great! I will talk to Diane. Do you fish, Porter?" asked Paulette as Porter was swallowing a huge gobble of pancake and dripping syrup.

"No, he grunted, "I don't like to fish! It's stupid!"

"Porter hasn't tried fishing yet. He doesn't realize what he's missing... He's from Florida." Ryan smiled at his "little dig" he had just given Porter.

"Just a second, I'll be right back." Paulette headed over and refilled the other restaurant guests' cups of coffee. Then she went over to the bookrack and selected a "Colorado Fly Fishing Guide" booklet. She handed it to Porter. "Here... I'll buy this for you. My treat. You should go fishing more often, Porter. It might help your sourpuss personality. Fishermen (and fisherwomen) are the happiest people you ever get to meet. You might want to try. Isn't that right, Mr. Downing?"

"I agree. I couldn't have said it any better. Just let me know when you and Diane want to come up. As I said, you are both welcome. I'm also glad to hear you are coming next Saturday to play music. I will look forward to that."

In the Jeep, Porter wondered, "Why is everyone picking on me...?"

Ryan turned up the volume on the Jeep CD player. Old time gospel bluegrass and country gospel tunes satiated the tone and atmosphere of the Jeep. Soon, the two travelers entered the busy maze of city traffic. Ryan guided the Jeep into the Albertson's shopping center parking lot. Customers were wheeling baskets of sacked groceries to their cars. It was busy. Ryan handed some cash to Porter in the back seat. "Here is $130.00. You can use this for your purchasing."

"What do you mean? Aren't you coming in, too?"

"No... sorry you left your shopping list at home. Keep track in your head how much you are spending. You decide what to buy. You are on your own. Since it's an hour drive back up to the cabin, I would suggest you save until last, picking out frozen foods and refrigerated items. When you finish, you can stop by that Panera Bread coffee shop a few shops down. I'm meeting Nathan there for a cup of coffee. I can introduce you."

Porter was instantaneously frustrated at this turn of events. Ryan climbed out of the Jeep and turned and walked away, towards the coffee shop. Porter stormed up to the entrance door of the grocery store. He grabbed one of the grocery carts. He pulled, but the shopping cart would not let loose from the other carts. Finally he jerked one cart loose from the pack. He stood there, both hands on the cart. "Now what do I do?" The money bulged in his right pocket.

"Hi Nathan... This is unusual. You beat me here. I'm usually first to be here."

"Hi, Ryan. How's the great old-man fisherman?" Nathan's friendly smile sparkled from his rotund face. His cheeks were always rosy, like a Santa Clause blush. He still had a very young look. He was a generation younger than Ryan. They were both good friends.

"I'll get my coffee."

He returned with his blend of hot water and coffee.

"Well Ryan, how's it going with your new visitor?"

"It's only been a week... but it seems like a month. We don't get along too well at the moment, but the situation is improving... I think."

"I thought you were bringing him along to introduce him to me. Did you leave him up at the cabin?"

"No, I have him doing the grocery shopping. He's shopping right now. I turned him loose on his own. No telling what he will buy. I had him make out a grocery list yesterday but he forgot it and left it home, so I'm making him shop without it."

"Why are you letting him choose which groceries to buy? I don't know of any fifteen-year olds who could handle that task very well."

"He needs experience in making good decisions. He needs to learn how to live with the consequences of his choices. I really don't know what to do with him. I just ask for help from the Lord every day to know what to do. Porter likes my movies, and I catch him beginning to read some of the books in my library, but he has a terrible, sourpuss, angry attitude. It will probably take a while for his anger to subside. An old man and an angry teenager, what a combination, huh?"

"You volunteered, remember?" reminded Nathan.

"Yep! I guess this is just another opportunity for my faith to grow. Can you believe that he doesn't even like to fish? I've started teaching him how to cook. I now have him washing the dishes every night. Bring me up to date, Nathan. How is your week going? How's the real estate market going for you?"

"I've really been busy this past week, showing houses. I'm getting a new listing this next week, and it looks like we are really getting close to offers with two of my buyers."

The two friends entered into catch-up chatter. Ryan liked his coffee mild and not strong. Nathan usually drank decaffeinated coffee or green tea. "Are you still planning on coming up Tuesday, Nathan?"

"Unless I'm writing an offer... It seems every time I make plans to go fishing I have an offer to deal with."

"Maybe you should plan more fishing trips then... it will help your business."

Porter pushed the grocery cart, filled with groceries, and parked beside the door into the coffee shop. He entered and found Ryan.

"Porter, this is Nathan. Nathan this is Porter." Porter's handshake was limp.

"I hear you don't like to fish... yet."

"No."

Ryan intervened. "Hope to see you Tuesday, Nathan. The big ones are waiting for you...if I don't get there first. I have pictures to prove it this time."

"Sure, sure, then how come you never catch a big one when I'm around?"

"I treat my guests royally, and I let you catch the big ones so you don't feel so badly. But this time I have pictures!"

"You ready, Porter? We better get back up the canyon."

"Nice to meet you Porter..." offered Nathan. Porter made a gentle wave gesture.

Nathan said, "See you next week."

After all the groceries had been loaded into the front seat, the two travelers returned up the winding canyon.

"Did you remember the toilet paper, Porter?"

"Yes. But when I got up to the register, the bill was too much for the cash I had. I had to start having the cashier take out items that I couldn't pay for. It was really embarrassing, with all those people standing around and

132

waiting on me to get finished so they could check out. How come you didn't help with the shopping? This isn't fair. This isn't my job! I'm not your maid!"

"Just think of it as a learning experience, Porter. Think of it as a trip into the wild allowing two strangers to survive another week or two in the wilderness. You had to make some decisions today. That's good experience. Now you and I have to live with the consequences of what you bought for us at the grocery store. Did you remember what those recipes called for? From now on, through the rest of your summer visit, you are responsible for all the grocery shopping. By the way, you haven't been keeping the firewood bins filled. That's another task that is entirely yours. And have you ever thought of saying 'Thank you' to Paulette for the fly fishing book she bought for you?"

For the evening meal, Porter fixed grilled ham and cheese sandwiches. He heated up some tomato soup out of a can and added crackers on the side. He added some Chili Cheese flavored Fritos. Porter poured some lemonade that he had mixed from a frozen can. Old man and teenager sat on the stools at the breakfast bar.

After supper, they both sat in the rocking chairs on the screened-in porch. As the dusk darkened into darkness, Ryan lit the wick in the Coleman Lantern that sat on the round table. The forest was extremely quiet. Seemingly, the only sounds were the reverberating creaks of the two rocking chairs. The moon was steadily climbing, illuminating the pine tree branches. Shadows again danced on the forest floor. The "swishing" "Blue Danube Waltz" still echoed in Porter's mind. The effortless sounds of restless crickets began. Ryan broke the stillness. "How about we start a fire in the fireplace and watch a movie?"

"OK."

"Do you have one you want to watch, Porter? Why don't you pick one out?"

"OK."

Porter selected, "Pretty in Pink," with Molly Ringwald. After the movie was over, Ryan turned to Porter. Tomorrow, I'm going to go over the ridge to Red Feather and fish a couple of lakes over there. On Sunday, sometimes, I have a favorite little restaurant I go to for breakfast and lunch. You are welcome to come along, if you want to."

"No," mumbled Porter.

# Chapter 16

Ryan guided the Jeep on the graveled road up over the hill and the ridge that separated Poudre Canyon from the Red Feather Lakes area. The trip was about ten miles from one canyon to the other. There was gorgeous mountain scenery along the way with huge boulders residing in the rolling green meadows. He figured that some glacier in the past had carried, and somehow deposited, these giant rocks. "How else could huge boulders end up in the middle of a meadow?"

On the right, He passed by the turnoff to the familiar old logging road. Before Quentin had given Ryan the cabin, Ryan often camped, off and on, all summer long. He especially enjoyed campsite 19, which was secluded from sight from the other scattered campsites. At several of his "low-in-spirit" times, he had even considered living in his camper, in the mountains, full-time. He had been depressed over his divorce, bankruptcy, and heart surgery. Just the sight of the logging road made him both sad and introspective. The peace and "time-spent" at the mountain campsite had helped Ryan regain some sense and purpose in life. Those were really tough times back then. He had "plowed" through those times. According to Ryan, "He had no other choice."

At the Red Feather Lakes Road, he turned the Jeep east. Then he turned north and headed to the Sportsman's

Café. It was a much smaller restaurant than Mountain Greenery. It was cozy with booths barely able to seat two big people across from each other. Four could fit in, but it was cramped. Outside the window where Ryan usually sat, were prairie dogs and small insect critters of all kinds, scurrying around. Almost everyone who came in the restaurant knew each other. The café was located on the road to Dowdy Lake where most of the tourist families fished on weekends. He sometimes fished Dowdy Lake during the week when there weren't as many people. He preferred fishing when no one else was around. That's one of the many reasons why he enjoyed his cabin so much. With the stream and the lake, he had his own private fishing haven.

He brought in his Bible and one of his most recently published books, "Pursuit of Peace Footsteps on the Bluegrass Gospel Jam Trail." With Porter being his cabin guest, He had been interrupted in his normal regular reading routine. In the mornings, he usually read ten chapters of the Bible and at least one chapter of his own books. He also carried a leather bound diary book that Nathan had given to him. Nathan wanted Ryan to record his experiences around each "Peace Book" that got distributed. Ryan had recently used the diary to record daily what was happening in his life. He often wrote down things he was thankful for. "It's amazing what can happen when you are thankful for what you have."

Ryan ordered his breakfast. The waitress recognized him.

"Nice to see you again. What are you up to today?"

"I don't know. I'm just relaxing and enjoying the surroundings. Just spending time getting peaceful."

"This is the place to do that. I'll put your order in... and bring you some more coffee."

"And a glass of ice water... too."

"OK."

Ryan prayed for God to illuminate his mind as he read the Bible verses. He prayed for guidance... Porter... and that He would know what to do in dealing with the troubled teen. He prayed for himself, too. He began his reading. By the time the breakfast arrived, he had read ten bible chapters from the book of James. Before eating the breakfast, he again prayed thanks to God for being healthy enough to eat this breakfast and enjoy it. He thanked God for his overall good health. He also prayed for God to help out with the gout that was beginning to develop in both of his feet, especially the right foot that was giving him extra pain. He sometimes had trouble hiking up to the lake and had to take it slower and slower each time. "I need extra help in dealing with Porter. Thank you, Lord."

Other breakfast guests started filing in, rapidly filling up the compact restaurant. Conversations soon filled the café. After breakfast, the waitress picked up the dishes and came back with the coffee pot and refilled his coffee mug.

Ryan started reading his "Footprints on the Gospel Jam Trail." He read two chapters, Chapter 6 and Chapter 7. As he was finishing, he placed his book on the table and picked up his restaurant ticket.

"More coffee?"

"No, I think I've had enough for the morning."

"What is that book you are reading?" The waitress picked up the book. The outside cover showed a log cabin sitting on the bank of a green and yellow beautiful lake.

"Oh, that's a book I wrote," answered Ryan.

'You wrote it? What's it about?"

"Peace. It's a Christian book based on my own personal experiences. I have authored six other books as well. Do you like to read?"

"Yes, reading is what I do a lot of when I'm up here for the summer."

"How about I give you this book as a gift? Here, let me sign it for you."

"No, I couldn't accept it. I would want to pay you for it. How much is it?"

"I tell you what," said Ryan, "I will give you this book... if... after you have read it and like it, you will pass it on to someone else."

"OK. I can probably do that." Ryan went up to the cashier counter and paid the ticket for the breakfast.

"Thanks for the book!"

"You are welcome."

Porter worked at tying another fly. This one turned out even uglier than the one he had tied yesterday. He became frustrated. He wandered over to the corner where Mr. Downing's library was located. He started reviewing all the books and titles. It was quite a varied assortment. Porter picked up "The Cross and the Switchblade," written by David Wilkerson. He went out to the porch and began reading. It was a story about a young preacher who was suddenly motivated by God to go to New York and preach to the gangs out there. Porter was amazed at how motivated an author would have to be, to dream up a story like this one. Nevertheless, in one sitting, he read the paperback book from beginning to end. At the end of the book, however, was a request to send in donations to, "Teen Challenge."

This printed request baffled Porter's mind. "Is this a true story?" he asked in his mind.

Later in the afternoon, Porter attempted tying another fly. He placed all his finished "ugly" flies in a zippered plastic sandwich bag. He planned out supper. He was preparing to fix steaks on the grill. He put in some potatoes in the oven to bake. He made a salad from lettuce, chopped up carrots, and chopped green onions. He cut up a tomato and placed it on the lettuce mound in the round bowl. He covered the salad with saran wrap. He set out some "Wishbone Italian Salad Dressing." He pulled out a bottle of "Heinz 57" steak sauce he bought yesterday. He placed the two medium steaks in a bowl filled with lemon marinating sauce. In one of the recipe books, it said that the potatoes could bake at 350 degrees for about an hour. With a fork, Porter began testing the potatoes every fifteen minutes to see if they were done. He brought out some margarine and some sour cream and placed the containers on the breakfast bar. He had never tasted sour cream but a lot of the recipes he read the other day included sour cream as an ingredient. "I'll surprise Mr. Downing with a full meal." For dessert, he planned on serving up a slice of the cherry pie he bought at the bakery.

Porter went outside and brought in more firewood and refilled the two firewood bins beside the fireplace. He prepared the coals inside the grill. He snatched another book from the Mr. Downing's library. He sat on the porch reading, "How to Win Friends and Influence People," by Dale Carnegie. Porter checked the baking potatoes. Finally his fork slid easily through the potato skins. He turned down the oven dial to "Warm." He continued his reading as he waited for Mr. Downing's return.

Ryan had been totally surprised and astounded at Porter's preparation of the steak and potatoes feast. Afterwards, Porter had even served up the cherry pie. Ryan brewed a pot of coffee. Ryan and Porter both sat in the clearing in folding chairs. They quietly gazed up at the stars that were beginning to brighten the approaching dark night. For about a half an hour, no conversation transpired.

"This is sure a balmy night, especially after that howling wind the other day," stated Ryan to start conversation.

"What howling wind?"

"The one you slept through like a log."

Porter offered no reply.

"I'm going to fish the stream tomorrow. Do you want to come along?"

"No."

"Nathan is coming up Tuesday. He should be up here around 9:00. We will probably fish on the stream most of the day. He usually ties a couple of new flies before we take off. He can show you some things about fly tying, if you want. We can have cereal and fruit for breakfast. How about we fix him a lunch to snack on? He usually doesn't stay for supper. He comes up three or four times a summer."

"OK."

# Chapter 17

Monday proceeded uneventfully. Ryan went fishing up the stream. The gout in his feet seemed to be letting up somewhat. Porter stayed at the cabin, reading more books and watching videos. Intermittently, Porter strolled around the clearing. His mind was experiencing some uncharacteristic kind of calmness. He started becoming aware of the weather. His inner feelings were genuinely interconnecting with the forest sounds. It was sort of a daunting feeling. He wasn't accustomed to these new types of thoughts. "Something must be going wrong, here," reflected Porter.

Porter guessed it was about 3:00, mid-afternoon. The wind stated swirling and gusting. Soon, gray clouds appeared and started gathering, obscuring the once-authoritative afternoon sun. Porter sat on the porch, observing. He could smell the fresh fragrance of rain. Soon a downpour ensued from the clouds. The rumbling thunder and lightning squall lasted for about twenty-five minutes. The mountain air had cooled. The gray overhead clouds dissipated. In next to no time, the afternoon sun was shining brightly again as if nothing was out of the ordinary. All of a sudden, the whole forest steamed upwards, like hot steaming coffee emanating out of a mug. It was an amazing transformation for Porter to observe. "I'll bet Mr. Downing got soaked," thought Porter.

"No, I just huddled underneath some big evergreen trees. I had my rain poncho with me, anyway. But that sudden rain made it slippery as I headed down the trail. It was like I was walking through streams running down the mountain. I waited under the evergreen branches until the trail streams slowed down. I hardly got wet. It was almost completely dry underneath those big evergreens. I had no other choice than to wait out the storm. It rains up here a lot in the afternoons. You just have to remember to be prepared. It is just part of nature opening up and speaking to you."

Porter thought, "I wonder if that's the feeling I was experiencing earlier?"

On Tuesday morning, Nathan's Honda car entered the clearing. Nathan was already decked out in olive green fishing gear. He put on his droopy fishing hat and his threadbare faded fishing vest. "Ready to go?" asked Nathan.

"Why don't you come on in and have some hot chocolate before we head up? Want some hot chocolate, Porter?"

"OK," replied Porter.

Nathan strolled past the fly-tying table. He picked up the zippered sandwich bag containing Porter's flies. "Been tying flies, Ryan?"

"No... not me." Ryan turned towards Porter. "Have you been tying flies, Porter?"

"Yeah, I tied some, but they are all ugly. They don't even look like the ones in the book."

"Why don't we try them today?" asked Nathan.

"But they are ugly!" replied Porter.

"Well," said Nathan, "there is a reason why they are in the water. Flies that are in the water always have something wrong with them... The pretty and perfect flies in the stores are designed to attract the fishermen's fancy. They don't always catch fish...but the flies are all very pretty. Let's try out your new pattern, Porter, and see what happens."

"I've never fished before."

"Come on, let's give it a try. Have you got some fishing gear for Porter?"

"Sure do, in that closet over there, down the hallway."

Before Porter had time to consider what he was doing, he found himself adorned with fishing gear.

"If these flies don't work, I'll help you tie some new ones when we get back," stated Nathan. To Ryan's amazement, Porter was agreeing to go fishing!

Ryan spoke up. "Nathan, why don't you and Porter fish the stream? I'll head up to the lake where I caught the big ones. Anyway, I need to rest in my camp chair. My back and feet have been giving me a little trouble. It works better, too, if only two people fish the stream, especially at the lower part. Three people make it a little crowded."

144

"Sounds good to me. How about you, Porter? I'll show you how to find the big ones, you know, the ones that Ryan can't seem to catch!"

Nathan showed Porter how to tie on one of Porter's "Ugly" flies to the end of the long clear tapered leader at the end of the heavier fly line. "We will try a few different fly patterns as we go. I have a good supply of flies."

All three of the fisherman grabbed the pre-prepared lunches that Porter had put together. Soon, Nathan and teenager started meandering up the trail beside the stream. Ryan headed up the trail to the lake. He wondered what just happened with Porter. "I guess when you pray to God, he answers in very mysterious ways."

Ryan had a very quiet restful day. He basked in both the hot sunshine and cool shade. The lake was serenely placid and unruffled. A fish surfaced, making a silent wide ring. As the afternoon dispelled into evening, He began experiencing strikes. They came fast, and he missed several fish. It was getting exciting now. He loved getting bites. The wind started shuffling across the surface of the lake, causing ruffles and rills. Quickly, a fish hit hard. Ryan jerked. He had a big one this time. He played the fish for several minutes, but then the fish was gone. He continued to throw out the bobber and fly, but it seemed that all the fish had gone to some other part of the lake. He had three more strikes, but it seemed like Ryan's timing was off. "At least, I got bites. It's still a good day."

Back at the cabin, the three fishermen gathered on the porch. Porter was genuinely excited and animated. Nathan had shown him some basic fly-casting techniques. "I caught a rainbow, one on my own fly," exclaimed Porter!

"Yep," agreed Nathan. "Looks like you have a secret weapon here, Ryan. It's been fun but I've got to get back to town." Before Nathan climbed back into his car, he turned to Porter and said, "Porter, why don't you tie some other patterns, too? You can start a whole new line of 'Ugly Flies by Porter.' Might be very profitable for you."

# Chapter 18

On Wednesday morning Mr. Downing and Porter headed to Mountain Greenery for breakfast.

"Coming to youth group tonight, Porter?" asked Paulette. "Do you want us to pick you up?"

"Yeah, OK, I guess..."

"Good, we will pick you up about the same time as before."

"How are you today, Mr. Downing?" asked Paulette. "What can I get for you? Want your normal order?"

"Porter, what do you want to order today?"

"The French Flapper."

"How do you want your eggs?"

"Scrambled, with a side order of bacon."

"Paulette returned with their orders. Ryan bowed his head and said a silent prayer. Porter waited.

About half way through breakfast, Porter suddenly spoke up and asked, "What's wrong with your feet?"

Surprised, Ryan spoke. "Oh last year, I had a really bad cold at the beginning of the year. I was so sick that I had to go to the hospital emergency room at 4:30 in the morning. They put me on some kind of water release treatment. A few weeks later, from my heart doctor, I found out that one of the side effects of the water treatment therapy, was the development of gout. It's a swelling in your extremities. I got it in both feet, especially my right foot. It was extremely painful. I could hardly wear my tennis shoes."

"You have a heart doctor?" asked Porter.

"Yes, I had double bypass heart surgery several years back."

"How come you hike up mountain trails if you have a bad heart?" inquired Porter.

"Well Porter, the heart condition I had... is called a 'widow maker.' Of the people who have the same heart condition as I had, fifty percent die before they get to the hospital. I was very fortunate. That's when I really decided to enjoy whatever it was that I was doing. I've lived by the motto, 'If I have to do anything, I'm going to choose something I enjoy doing.'"

Ryan paused. He continued, "That's why I write. That's why I do Bluegrass Gospel Jams. That's why I let God have control of my life. That's why I pray and turn each day over to God. I pray for you, too, Porter."

"More coffee, Mr. Downing?" interrupted Paulette.

Porter acquiesced into silence.

"Been getting any fishing in, Mr. Downing?" asked Paulette.

"Yes, as a matter of fact, I have. Even Porter, here, went fishing for the first time yesterday... and he actually caught a fish with a fly that he tied from scratch."

"That's amazing," said Paulette. "What kind of fly did you tie, Porter?"

"An 'ugly fly.' It didn't look very good... but I caught a fish. It was actually a very fun experience." Porter's answer was an energized response, surprising both Ryan and Paulette.

Teenager and old man returned to the cabin. Ryan started writing on his laptop computer. Porter silently attempted more fly patterns. Soon Porter had three more flies tied. Ryan got up from the computer for a glass of water. Porter spoke up suddenly. "Would it be all right to borrow that mandolin for tonight? I think I might try to learn how to play it, with the group."

"Sure, Porter. There's a mandolin case in that closet with all the fishing gear. I don't know how to play the mandolin, so I can't show you. If you ever want to play guitar, I can show you some basic chords, but I don't know anything about a mandolin."

"There's a guy named Jeff in the youth group who plays. I think he might show me. He just started playing about a month ago. But he's really good."

Paulette's group arrived at 5:15. Porter strolled out to the Jeep. He placed the mandolin and case along with the other instrument cases. Porter positioned himself in the back seat. He had the Living Bible in his right hand. He placed it by his feet. Soon the Jeep and the passengers proceeded merrily out of the clearing.

At the church, Jeff began showing Porter how to tune the mandolin. Then he showed Porter three basic chords.

"If you learn these three chords, you can play along with just about any song," said Jeff. "It takes some practice, but the fastest way to learn is to play along with a group, like we are doing tonight. I'm looking forward to playing and jamming at your place this Saturday. I had to get special permission to come. I think it will be a lot of fun. I can show you more then. Try and practice some on your own."

"How come you have to get special permission?"

"I'll let you know sometime."

"How do you know when you are supposed to change finger positions?" asked Porter.

Jeff explained, "You listen and hear the word where the song changes and watch the fingers of another mandolin player. Sit right across from me and follow. You have to listen to the words and watch my fingers. Don't worry about fancy picking. That will come later. It takes a while to learn the finger positions."

"But I don't even know the songs you guys are playing."

"You just have to learn. Sean has a chord book with words and chords above the words. That's how I learned."

Sean spoke up. "Who has a Bible verse to share tonight?" Each of the seven other participants shared a Bible verse, making a comment each time. It was Porter's turn.

"Do you have a Bible verse you would like to share, Porter," asked Sean.

Porter paused... "No..."

"That's OK," said Sean. "Let's get started! Let's fill up this church with some rousing gospel music! And remember... we are having a good old time bluegrass jam at Porter's house this coming Saturday. What time, Porter?"

"I think at 6:30." Mr. Downing had sketched out a map and made copies for Porter to hand out. "Uh...uh... I have a map for anyone who needs directions... Paulette knows the way."

# Chapter 19

It was now Saturday morning. Ryan and Porter arrived at Mountain Greenery around 8:30. The restaurant was bubbling with conversations and activity. About the same time, Diane walked in. "I hear we are having a jam tonight at your house, Porter."

"Yeah..."

"Are you meeting anyone for breakfast, Diane?" asked Mr. Downing.

"No, I just drove up last night and I didn't feel like cooking this morning."

"Would you like to join Porter and me?"

"OK." Diane sat down, next to Porter. Porter shifted over. He wasn't used to sitting close to a member of the female species. Paulette came by to take everyone's breakfast order.

Paulette spoke, "Our whole group is excited about coming up for the jam tonight. I think a lot of people will be there. Do you have room for all of us, Mr. Downing?"

"I have lots of folding chairs we can set up."

"I've been inviting just about everyone I know." added Paulette. "Even the director of the Ranch where Jeff works said he might come, too. He said he might come later. I think he plays the banjo."

"We are happy to have you all come," replied Mr. Downing. Turning to Diane, he said, "Paulette tells me that you and Paulette like to fish. Why don't you both come up to the cabin this next week? You can fish the stream, or hike up to the lake."

"Yes, Polly told me. We both have Tuesday off. How about then?"

"Sure, that will work. Maybe even Porter will show you his new 'Ugly' flies that he caught fish with the other day.

Paulette overheard and remarked slyly, "Might have a new fisherman being born..."

Breakfasts were delivered by Paulette. Mr. Downing and Diane bowed their heads. Porter waited. Most of the conversation flowed back and forth between Diane and Mr. Downing.

Ryan. "Are you an author, Mr. Downing?"

"Yes, I am. I've written six books so far. I'm working on book seven now."

"I've heard they are Christian books. Is that right?"

"Well, replied Ryan, "The first one was written about how to use a computer in real estate. Yes, the other books are all Christian books about the 'Pursuit of Peace.' They are based on my true experiences with God. When you come up Tuesday, I'll show them to you. I have a library up at my cabin. I have a new book just out, 'Bluegrass Gospel Jams.'"

"That would be great!" replied Diane, "Fishing and 'Pursuit of Peace...' ... sounds like those two topics mix together pretty well. Bluegrass gospel jams, too?"

"Yes, I think so."

Porter's body crumpled in the booth, his lanky frame wanting to retreat from this conversation. He offered no participation, except to answer a few direct questions from Diane. His answers were short and stiff. Porter was internally wrestling with different emotions that were now surfacing more and more often.

Diane spoke up. "Porter, are you going to play mandolin tonight? Jeff said you were catching on very fast. Mr. Downing, what instrument do you play?"

"Guitar."

"I play fiddle," added Diane.

Porter and Mr. Downing returned to the cabin. "I'm going to relax at the lake this afternoon," announced Ryan. "Do you think you can prepare for the group without me? Have you planned out what you are serving as far as refreshments? Can you set up some chairs in a circle? There are extra chairs in the storage shed out back."

"Yes," replied Porter. I can handle that. I'm baking some chocolate fudge brownies. I'm fixing coffee and lemonade and ice water. We have a variety of cookies we can set out. I thought we would get a fire going."

"Good." He was amazed at Porter's response. Ryan donned his fishing gear, slung the green-sleeved folding chair over his shoulder, and hiked up towards the lake.

Porter remained at the cabin. He started organizing the living room and kitchen bar. He placed the chairs in a semi-circle around the fireplace. He moved the couch over towards the library. Soon he had room for about fifteen people. He then began preparing and baking the brownies. At the store last week, he had purchased two boxes of devil's food double chocolate chewy brownies. He had trouble finding two different baking pans to cook with, but he looked around until he came up with two pans that would work. He found a large mixing bowl below the kitchen cabinet. He retrieved a spatula from the silverware drawer and proceeded to make the brownie mixture. He diligently followed every step in the directions on the box, adding eggs and canola oil. He set the oven timer. Soon the aroma of salubrious baking brownies permeated the kitchen and the whole cabin. Porter ambled over to Mr. Downing's library. This time he picked up, "The Power of Positive Thinking," by Norman Vincent Peale. As he previewed the pages, he thought, "Huh... another book by a preacher..."

Ryan returned to the cabin. His fishing excursion was both profitable and peaceful. His feet didn't even bother him. He found Porter sitting on the porch, reading... Inside, Ryan found the cabin all prepared and ready for the expected visitors. The aroma of baked brownies still lingered. He was surprised again that Porter had taken the initiative to do something on his own. Ryan warmed up some spaghetti and sauce, poured a cup of coffee, and headed out to the porch. Porter was still engrossed in his reading. It appeared that Porter was about halfway through "The Power of Positive Thinking." Ryan said nothing. A quiet mood settled upon the porch. The wind stilled to a whisper.

Soon, cars and SUVs started coming into view. Vehicles all started to show up all about the same time, one after another. Ryan introduced himself to each visitor. Sean and his wife, Kristin, introduced themselves. Each one of the visitors carried an instrument case. Porter showed them into the great room where the chairs were set up. Porter got the fire started. Teenagers and adults started filling up the cabin. Porter went out to the storage shed and retrieved more chairs. Each of the musicians seemed to know what to do. They brought in their music stands. There were about double the number of musicians than were at the church last Wednesday night. As the musicians' gathering grew, a tune started spontaneously, with Paulette's banjo leading the way. Ryan found a spot on the end of the musician semicircle so he could watch and welcome people in. He had tuned his guitar earlier. Porter, with his borrowed mandolin, sat next to Jeff at the other end. Within a few minutes, the group started taking turns choosing the songs. The cabin surged and bulged with peppy fast-moving good old-time bluegrass gospel and church tunes.

Ryan smiled inwardly. He always wanted this cabin to be a place where he could host bluegrass gospel jams in the mountains. Now, it was actually happening. One of his goals was now evolving into existence. An answer to prayer was manifesting itself right before his eyes. When it came time for Ryan to choose his first song, he chose, "Unclouded Day." Effortlessly, Paulette and her banjo began the rousing song. All the musicians joined in. They took turns with instrumental breaks, fiddle breaks, harmonica breaks, mandolin breaks, and even an autoharp break. When it came time for Jeff's turn, he led off with, "I'm Using My Bible For A Road Map." Sean and Kristin played and sang, "Old Country Church."

Ryan greeted and welcomed each new person as other visitors continued to drop in. About thirty minutes later, a tall man with a brown leather cowboy hat strolled in. He had a banjo case with him. He gripped Ryan's hand. "Hi, I'm Hayden Price. My ranch is about five miles up the canyon. Jeff works for me. I know Paulette from the restaurant. Got room for another banjo player?"

"Sure do. How do you spell, 'Hayden,' 'h a y d e n?" He always tried to purposely remember the new visitor's name.

"Yes."

"Glad to meet you. You are welcome to join in. Just find a place to squeeze in."

"OK."

For Ryan, this was truly a heavenly gathering. Music always restored and raised his soul and spirit to a new pinnacle. This evening was no exception. He observed Porter. Porter was actually trying to figure out chords on the mandolin. Ryan gathered together some of the 3-hole ring binder songbooks he had in a pile. He passed them out to the musicians and spectators. He added a couple of wood chunks onto the fire.

Someone chose, "Farther Along," one of Ryan's favorite slow songs. The unrehearsed harmony of that group had an intrinsic beauty. The cowboy, "Hayden," chose "Foggy Mountain Breakdown." It was difficult to keep up with Hayden's high-speed rhythm. Everyone was smiling and laughing and having a good time.

The jam continued with everyone taking turns and participating. Sean encouraged the spectators to choose songs. Someone in the jam always seemed to know whatever song was chosen. The rest of the musicians followed along, catching the beat and following the bluegrass rhythm of the songs. In the middle of the jam, Ryan suggested having a refreshment break for about ten to fifteen minutes. He knew that this activity was one of the most important times... time to get acquainted with each other. He took his brownie and lemonade out to the porch. Hayden also came out to the porch with a cup of coffee and a brownie. He had to stoop so his cowboy hat wouldn't hit the doorway header He sat in the other rocking chair across from Ryan.

"This is really nice of you to open up your home to a group like this, Mr. Downing. I'm really enjoying myself. It looks like everyone else is having a great time, too."

"Call me, Ryan. Yes, this is one of my goals coming into fruition. I could do this every week and never get tired."

"Is Porter your grandson?"

"No, he's my guest for the summer. He's the great grandson of a very good friend of mine, Quentin Paisley. Quentin actually gave this cabin to me. When I was requested to let Porter stay up at the cabin for a couple of months, I said, 'yes.' I don't really have much experience dealing with a troubled teenager. I just keep saying prayers every day."

"He appears to be enjoying this gathering," answered Hayden. "He and Jeff have suddenly seemed to become good friends. Jeff has a troubled past, too. He came to the ranch about a month ago. He is rapidly beginning to develop a positive personality. I gave him that mandolin that used to belong to my dad. Since then he has been taking it to youth group and playing it on Wednesday nights. Sean, the youth group leader at the Chapel of the Pines got Jeff started. Sean plays about five different instruments, very talented guy. The youth group came over and did a concert for us at the ranch. Paulette and Diane were the ones who actually invited Jeff to the youth group. They give

159

him a ride every week. He seems to be emerging out of his angry shell. It's sure a lot different than when he first came to the ranch."

"What kind of ranch do you operate?"

"It's a ranch for handicapped kids. Different organizations sponsor visits for kids with handicaps. We teach them how to ride a horse and how to act in a positive way towards others. It's a very rewarding experience. We use teenagers to help with each of the kids. When we get an angry or misguided teenager to help with the handicapped kids, then an amazing phenomenon begins happening. The partnership starts benefiting both. For the first time, Jeff has actually acquired some normalcy, simply based on helping others. I'm really amazed that Jeff is helping Porter learn the mandolin. This is a definitely a positive turnaround in his personality."

"I'm surprised that Porter seems to be doing a turnaround, too, just the beginning," said Ryan.

"Jeff works for me all week long. Saturdays are our busiest times and we are short handed right now. Do you think Porter would come and help out on Saturdays? We don't pay the teenagers a wage. They get credits two for one for each hour they work. We pay the state for the hours they work. We wouldn't be able to put Porter on the payroll, but we could set it up so that Porter would be assisting Jeff. Jeff would get additional credits just for Porter helping out. Maybe we could foster a friendship between the two."

"Well, I am running out of ideas to keep a restless teenager occupied. I have just now got him interested in fly-fishing. I think helping out handicapped kids would be a good idea. Why don't you ask Porter and Jeff tonight what they think about the situation?"

"OK," answered Hayden. "If you could give Porter a ride to the ranch on Saturday mornings, I would see to it that he gets a ride back to your place Saturday evening."

"Sounds good to me. We can both pray that the two teenagers don't affect each other in a negative way. It's a risk, but I feel that Porter needs a friend. Maybe the mandolin is the key. By the way, why is Jeff up here at your ranch?"

"He and some of his friends vandalized a school. He's attempting to give restitution for what he did. The judge sent him to us. What happened with Porter?"

"Something similar... Porter will have to tell you when he is ready."

"I will talk to them both after the jam. This is sure good coffee."

"Porter made it... and the brownies."

# Chapter 20

Paulette refilled Mr. Downing's coffee mug.

"We sure had a good time jamming at your cabin last night, Mr. Downing. Where's Porter this morning?"

"Still sleeping. He hasn't quite got used to getting up early... on a consistent basis. The jam was a great time for me, too. We will have to do another jam sometime soon. I think everyone had a good time. Thanks for inviting Hayden. We had never met before."

"Hayden?"

"Yes, the banjo player with the cowboy hat."

"Oh. Yes, Mr. Price. He usually comes in almost every day in the early afternoon just before we close and has coffee and pie. He is a very friendly person, easy-going, and gentle. You wouldn't think he runs a ranch for misguided and troubled teenagers."

"A boat is safe in the harbor. But this is not the purpose of a boat."

"I like your new saying. Did you make up that one on your own?"

"No," answered Paulette. "I got that one out of a Guidepost Magazine."

"This last issue? I haven't read this month's issue. That's my favorite reading. The articles always pick up my spirits. I read that magazine all the time, every month, cover to cover."

"Me, too," said Paulette. "In the jeep on the way back last night, Jeff said Porter was going to go up and help Jeff out next Saturday at the ranch. I think that's great."

"I'm curious, why you think that's great?'

"Well, at first, Jeff... when I first met him here at the restaurant, was very bitter and angry... a lot like Porter. But then in just a couple of short weeks, his attitude suddenly changed. The youth group went over and played music for all the handicapped kids. Mr. Price gave Jeff that mandolin that used to belong to Mr. Price's own father. That's when Jeff started coming to youth group. I think that working at the ranch, and learning how to play that mandolin, have given him a whole new perspective on life. I think his real self, down deep, is coming out now. It's an amazing transformation, becoming a normal person."

"You sure do have an introspection insight on life and people," commented Ryan. "How did you develop that skill so well?

"Experience...a lot of experience, I guess. I used to be the fat girl, all through junior high and senior high. I was a big-boned specimen. Everyone used to call me, 'Polly the Parrot...Polly want a cracker?' I was excluded and ignored by everyone, except Diane. She has always been my best friend. Even when I started losing weight by exercising and eating less the last couple of years, no one wanted to be around me. I didn't want to be around them, either. Then when I got this waitress job, and the one I got in my senior year, I found I enjoyed talking to people and making them feel good. Now, everyone talks to me. In my own way, I think I got transformed, too."

"Well, you certainly are a pleasant personality. You make my breakfast times special."

Paulette's face flushed red for a moment. "Thank you. Want your usual?"

Ryan slowly devoured his "Farmer's Son" breakfast, relishing every bite. The hubbub conversation of the restaurant started gathering momentum as more and more Sunday morning guests started filing in. Many folks smiled at Ryan and said, "Hello." Maybe he was smiling at them. So many smiles... he must be outwardly smiling internally. Paulette returned with Mr. Downing's meal check. "Don't forget...you and Diane are coming up Tuesday to go fishing!"

"We are planning on it. Thanks for coming in."

When he returned to the cabin, the lanky teenager was still asleep. Ryan started writing. He was energized by his recent breakfast conversation with Paulette.

Finally, Porter slowly arose and went into the kitchen and fixed some instant oatmeal from a packet. He poured a large glass of orange juice and went out to the porch and sat down. He picked up the book he had been reading yesterday. He became engrossed in the words. Ryan entered the porch.

"I'm going to fish the lake. Want to come along?"

"No, I think I'll stay here."

"Did you enjoy the jam last night, Porter? You looked like you were having a good time."

"Yes, Jeff showed me a lot of things on the mandolin. I just need to practice some more. But I don't know any of the songs everyone was playing."

"Just a minute, Porter." Mr. Downing went inside the cabin and returned with a CD. "Here is a CD with a lot of the songs we were playing last night. There's a mandolin playing that you would probably be able to follow along with. Most of the songs are very basic chords."

"Thanks, I'll try it. Oh, and thanks for setting me up to go next Saturday to help Jeff at his ranch job."

"That was Mr. Price's idea. He seems like a very nice person."

"Yes, he is very gentle... and... congenial." Porter smiled slightly at his own little "word dig" towards Mr. Downing.

Ryan headed up the trail to the lake. The songs from last night's jam reverberated in his mind.

# Chapter 21

Tuesday arrived. Paulette and Diane hopped out of the Jeep. "We are ready for fishing!" said Diane.

"Hello, Mr. Downing," greeted Paulette.

"Would you girls like some hot chocolate before you head up?"

"No, thanks." replied Paulette, "We already had breakfast." Porter entered the porch.

"You are coming fishing with us, aren't you, Porter? How come you're not ready to go? The fish are anxiously awaiting us. Where are those famous flies you said that were so good? We need a guide to show us where to fish. Hurry up and let's get going. The morning is dwindling away... Are you coming Mr. Downing?"

"Why don't you three fish the stream? I'm going up to the lake where I can sit in my chair and fish... I do a lot of my writing in my mind. Fishing is always a peaceful pastime for me. When you three return, I'll have a spaghetti supper for you. I make an excellent spaghetti sauce."

The peer pressure was on again. Porter retreated into the cabin and put on the fishing gear. He took his "Ugly" flies and placed the plastic bag in his fishing vest pocket. He grabbed three apples and three tangelos from the fruit bowl on the counter and placed the fruit into the inside zippered vest pocket. Paulette and Diane stood in the open clearing and waited. Mr. Downing pointed towards the trail entrance behind the cabin. "Porter knows the way. Just follow that path by the stream. The first stretch is fairly tough to fish, but when you get up a ways, it levels out. I call it, 'High Mountain Meadow.' There is also a large pool under a huge rock I call, 'Cascade Pool.' If you sneak up on the pool, you can almost always pull one or two out. The stream actually traces all the way back up to the lake. I haven't fished that upper part of the stream. It's pretty steep and challenging. One of these days, I intend to hike up all the way."

Porter entered the clearing. "OK. I'm ready."

"Here Porter," said Mr. Downing. "Take my camera along with you. Put it in that other zippered pouch."

Encouraged, "Let's go," offered Paulette. She took the lead. Diane followed Paulette. Porter followed Diane. Ryan was amazed yet again that Porter was actually going fishing. The trio disappeared from view. Ryan pondered, "How come I can't get Porter to go fishing? He goes with others... But that's all right... At least he is doing something on his own."

Ryan went inside. He decided to prepare the spaghetti sauce and to let it simmer all day. In the electric skillet, he browned two one-pound packages of hamburger. He retrieved half of a red onion from the refrigerator and chopped it up with a serrated knife. He mixed in the onions with the cooking hamburger. He opened a large can of tomato sauce and then added two cans of spicy diced tomatoes He added some garlic powder and some Italian spices from a bottle. He stirred the mixture. The last step was to add "Cholula" Mexican hot sauce and some Worcestershire sauce. The spaghetti sauce started bubbling. He stirred the sauce and turned down the electric skillet to "Simmer." The kitchen filled with the spicy aroma. He tasted the sauce with a small spoon. "Needs just a little more Cholula hot sauce... Ahh... good..."

Ryan went over to his CD collection and put on Andre Rieu, "La vie est belle" (Life is Beautiful). He turned up the volume. Suddenly, he didn't feel like going fishing. He was enjoying the solitude peace of his mountain cabin. He reclined in his chair for a long while, savoring the music and the simmering odor of the spaghetti sauce. He realized that he had had no solitary solitude times since Porter had arrived. Porter was always present and on his mind. Now he had the cabin to himself again. He decided to enjoy the peacefulness of his own thoughts. "Who knows? I might even do some more writing today." Ryan felt drowsy.

He began dozing in his chair. He slept for almost an hour. He awoke refreshed. He replayed the CD. Ryan went out to the porch, "Diet 7-Up" in hand. He sipped on the cold drink. He snacked on some salted peanuts that he had recovered from the kitchen pantry. The wind was warm, caressing the porch. The Andre Rieu orchestra filled the stillness of the forest. Ryan was home. Ryan was peaceful. Ryan was thankful. Across the clearing, two cow elk strolled across the clearing and into the evergreens. "This path past the cabin must be a game trail."

Soon, Ryan was busy at his computer, composing. He composed until the late afternoon. His time was productive. He finished writing one chapter and started another. Later, he watched the movie, "October Sky," about three teenagers from Virginia building rockets right after the Russians launched "Sputnik," the first man-made satellite ever to orbit the earth. On the DVD were the actual "Rocket Boys" who related all the truth in the movie. The movie was based on true facts.

Ryan played another Andre Rieu CD, "Masterpieces." He especially enjoyed, "Amazing Grace," played by the whole orchestra and a combined huge bagpipe orchestra. Ryan relished the soul-stirring music. He kept the volume high and sat and sipped coffee on the porch. In the late afternoon, the girls and Porter returned. Their stride was brisk and spirited. Even Porter followed at the brisk pace.

"How did you do?" asked Mr. Downing.

"Great..." replied Paulette. "That's a terrific place to fish! It's so beautiful, too. I caught eight."

"I caught five," added Diane. "Four others got off. I caught one with Porter's 'Ugly' fly!"

"How many did you catch, Porter?"

"Zip. I was busy taking pictures with the camera."

"Come on in and have some spaghetti. All I have to do is to boil the spaghetti noodles and warm up the garlic French bread. We have fresh strawberries and ice cream for dessert. You guys can wash up in the bathroom sink."

Paulette strolled over to the library on the far wall. "Where are your books, the ones you wrote?" asked Paulette. Diane came over and stood by Paulette.

"On the bottom shelf..."

"Are all these books on the 'Pursuit Of Peace?" asked Diane.

"Yes, you can select whichever ones you want," replied Mr. Downing, "to take with you... My newest book is there, too."

Porter joined in with the conversation. "You mean you published all of these books? You wrote all of them?"

"Yep."

"Can Paulette and I borrow two apiece? We can share them back and forth."

"Sure," said Mr. Downing, "Let's all have some spaghetti."

The three teenagers and Mr. Downing sat in silence at the table. Mr. Downing turned and asked Paulette if she would pray for the meal. The three of them bowed their heads. Paulette said a prayer. Porter sat and waited, eyes open, pondering the situation. Paulette finished her prayer with, "Thank you Lord for this wonderful day, for Mr. Downing's hospitality, a beautiful fishing spot, and for

Porter's 'Ugly' fly that Diane caught that German Brown with today. Amen." Chuckles followed the prayer.

"Diane, you caught a German Brown?" inquired Mr. Downing.

"I have pictures!" piped in Porter.

"Maybe you girls should come up again. Porter can tie some more flies"

"Can we come up again next Tuesday? asked Diane.

"Sure! Is that OK with you, Porter?" asked Mr. Downing.

"Sure..."

# Chapter 22

A routine started settling in. Porter began regularly accompanying Ryan to the consistent restaurant breakfasts. On Tuesdays, Paulette, Diane, and Porter fished. On one Tuesday, Nathan came up again. He and Ryan hiked up to the lake while the teenagers fished the stream. Porter was developing into the evening cook, fixing hamburgers, chicken, and steaks on the grill. Porter had taken over the grocery shopping as well. Friday became grocery-shopping day. Porter searched and found new recipes to try out. Ryan went out for coffee with Nathan in town on Friday mornings while Porter shopped. The morning coffee appointments with Quentin diminished. Quentin was not doing well. He didn't feel like getting out to a restaurant.

Every Wednesday evening, Porter went with the youth group and began joining in and playing the mandolin. On Saturdays, Porter went up to the ranch and helped Jeff. One weekday, Porter surprised Ryan by hiking up the trail to the lake all by himself. Porter wanted to try out some new flies he had created. He caught three fish that day. He took pictures with Ryan's borrowed camera. Ryan became productive in his writing output, enjoying the quiet times when Porter was vacant from the cabin.

Porter started practicing the mandolin. Porter often read the books from Ryan's library. He also began reading the "Pursuit of Peace" books that Ryan had authored. He continued to watch more DVD movies. One movie of special interest to Porter was, "Facing the Giants," about a high school football coach who continually had a losing season until he turned over to God, the purpose of the team. Porter watched that movie three times. Eventually, Ryan, on his guitar, and Porter, on his mandolin, began playing gospel songs together.

Another Jam developed at the cabin one Saturday night. Word had gotten around the little mountain canyon. This time, fifteen musicians showed up, along with about fifteen spectators. The cabin was packed with music and people. Diane had invited most everyone she knew. She requested that each person bring some "goodies" to munch on. Porter and Jeff began taking mandolin breaks together on the songs. Porter had rapidly caught on and was speedily becoming a participating member of the gospel jam. Ryan noticed that Porter was beginning to smile occasionally. At the halfway point in the jam, Hayden and Ryan went out to the porch and sat in the rocking chairs and sipped coffee. "Can you believe what's happening with Jeff and Porter?" asked Hayden.

"Looks like a miracle in the making," responded Ryan. "I am amazed that Porter has enjoyed the Saturdays at your ranch. I thought he would have a hard time working with your handicapped kids."

"He is good with them. One of the kids, Gary, ten years old, on Porter's first day, smacked Porter in the mouth. He is a very angry kid. Porter sat him down and set him straight. Now, Gary has been a little easier to get along with. It seems Porter has established some sort of boundary for Gary to respect."

"Truly amazing," commented Ryan.

Hayden replied, "Yes, and another kid named, Steven, seems to have become attached to Porter. Porter just gravitates towards helping out. He relates well to the kids. He helps the kids ride the horses. In between rides, he uses and demonstrates his mandolin to them. Jeff also says Porter has really begun playing up a storm at youth group."

"Porter's attitude around here has definitely improved. I wasn't so sure of that at the beginning. I was beginning to think I had made a mistake by letting him come up and visit. I guess, when you pray, God answers in mysterious ways."

"I can go along with that! I'm going to miss not having Jeff and Porter around. Jeff only has two more weeks up here before he has to leave and go back home."

"Where is Jeff's 'home'?" asked Ryan.

"Sterling, Colorado."

"Porter is going back in two weeks to Tampa, Florida."

"I hear the fishing is good up here at your cabin," said Hayden.

"Yep... mighty good. Would you like to come up and go fishing?"

"I might just do that. It's hard to take a day off right now."

"Come up late in the afternoon. The days are getting longer. Fishing at the lake is good at that time of day. I have fishing gear if you need it."

"No, I have my own. I've just been too busy to go fishing."

"No one should be too busy to go fishing!" smiled Ryan.

Ryan and Hayden rejoined the music inside the cabin.

# Chapter 23

On Monday morning, at breakfast at Mountain Greenery, Porter unexpectedly became talkative. He started peppering Ryan with questions. "Do you really believe all that stuff in your books or is that something you just dreamed up in your mind?"

"Which books?"

"Those 'Pursuit of Peace' books. Are they real or fiction?"

"What makes you think they aren't real, Porter"

"I don't know. I get a strange feeling when I read them."

"What kind of feeling?"

"I don't know... it seems like someone is close by, whispering over my shoulder. It's eerie."

"Maybe an angel is trying to get your attention, Porter."

"An angel?"

"Yes, I've had that same experience at different times in my life. I think God talks to us as we travel life's roads, especially when we reach roadblocks and troubles of some kind. You are just experiencing some answers to prayers."

"I haven't been praying and asking God for anything!" answered Porter, demandingly.

"Other people have been praying for you, Porter. It's not all about you and your prayers for yourself. I've been praying for you. I suspect that the judge who sent you here has been remembering you in her prayers. I suspect that Sean and the youth group have been praying for you. I believe that your dad and great grandpa, Quentin, have been praying for you. God sometimes talks to us in different and mysterious ways."

"So do you really believe that stuff you write about?" asked Porter.

"I wouldn't have written those books if I didn't believe. I am an encourager. I want as many people as possible... to believe. There is no 'true peace' in this world without God. He created all this mountain majesty around us. He created both you and me in his image. Those bible verses in my books help me, and others, stay on course with a bountiful life. You know, Porter, you don't have to go through life angry all the time. There is a better way of living. From what I have observed, you are just beginning to figure out that part."

Porter pondered for a while, his thoughts focusing on how to respond to Mr. Downing's answer. "I have watched that movie, 'Facing the Giants,' three times now. Is that a fictional or an actual true story?"

"I'm sure the story is fictional, but all the bible facts presented are actual. The movie portrays what can happen when you turn things over to God. A church made that

177

movie. The movie was made so they could reach out and help people believe in God. I think it was designed to have a real impact... on both teenagers... and adults. I think it has a tremendous impact on my life, too. I'm always motivated after I watch it. My mental battery gets recharged every time."

"Recharged? What does that mean?" asked Porter.

"Well, Porter, we always walk around as mortal beings. All of us need reminders to help stay the course of fruitful living. That's what bible verses do for me. I need reminders all the time. That's why I read the bible. I believe the bible and what it says. That's the reason I put my favorite bible verses in my books, so that others can be encouraged to live a bible-based life of victory. I am energized and recharged in my heart when I see answers to prayers manifest in peoples' lives. You are manifesting a prayer answer right now. I wasn't so sure when you first came. I didn't even begin to know how to deal with you."

"Why did you let me come up here?" demanded Porter, sternly.

"To help out a very good friend... but I did pray first. Your great grandpa Quentin and I are great good friends. I met him when he first came to the Bluegrass Gospel Jams. That's where we first met. He took one of my original peace booklets home. He also gave a huge $100.00 contribution, at least huge to me. You might remember to say thanks to him before you go back to Florida. You know, Porter, a lot of people are trying to help you, even people you probably don't know about. How about Mr. Price? Jeff? Paulette and Diane? Sean? The youth group? Your dad? The Judge? Have you said 'thanks' to any of those people?"

Porter pondered, but answered indirectly, "Yeah, but you don't know how I grew up. You never experienced all the crap I've had to go through. All that my mother ever does is to yell at me. My dad never says anything. He never speaks up. He never even tries."

"Let me ask you a question, Porter, Who do you think was responsible for your coming up here to the mountains instead of jail? Ryan let his question linger. "That's right, your dad!"

"But, but... He never did before... all this time. And my mom... she never..."

"And so, now, you are going to blame all your bad actions on the way your family raised you? You don't think you had any part in choosing how to react? Is everyone else to blame? Who are you, Porter? Who do you want to be? You know you do have a choice."

"Are you saying I should become a 'Christian' and believe in all that bible stuff?"

"Sure. But neither I, nor anyone else, can make that choice for you. That has to be your own decision. You should be thankful that the Judge and your Dad sent you here. Can't you now begin to see that it is possible to make a course correction and begin living in a better and more prosperous way?"

"You mean money?"

"No, I mean living a life of true peace and enjoying life... instead of fighting life. In the bible it says, '... to do unto others what you would have them to do unto you.' It also says to 'give and you will receive.' You can have a wonderful life, Porter, if you just decide to have it that way."

Porter ate his breakfast in silence. Ryan pondered about where these words of wisdom were coming from.

On Tuesday, Paulette, Diane, and Porter hiked up the trail all the way to the far end of the stream where it became too hard to traverse. They started fishing the holes on the way down. Porter's mind-thoughts were enmeshing with the naturalness of the mountain surroundings. He was actually developing a sense of peacefulness. He had never noticed beauty before. It seemed like the sun was illuminating hidden previously ignored observations. He found himself actually enjoying this new unfolding nature scene.

Ryan drove into town later that morning and met Quentin for a late breakfast.

"How's my great grandson doing?" asked Quentin in his low gravely voice. The tube from the oxygen bottle encircled his head and nose.

"Better and better, I think. He is up fishing today with two friends, actually they are girls. We had our very first meaningful conversation a couple of days ago. How are you doing health-wise?"

"About the same as before... I'm still going to kick the bucket pretty soon...it's coming. I would like to see my great grandson before I go... maybe I'll last for another couple of weeks."

"I'll encourage him to visit you before he goes back to Florida."

"Thanks, Ryan. You have been a very good friend to me. I appreciate it."

"And you have been a very good friend and encourager to me, too."

# Chapter 24

On Wednesday morning, Ryan and Porter arrived at the restaurant around 9:00 AM. The restaurant was almost vacant. Paulette sat down at their table. Her bushy brown eyebrows bounced up and down. Paulette began excitedly, "We hiked up all the way to the top of the trail yesterday. Did Porter tell you about it? The fishing was excellent. I think Diane and I caught about six fish each. Porter even caught some." Paulette smiled, glancing over towards Porter.

"Did you use the 'Ugly' flies?" asked Ryan.

"Yeah," replied Paulette, "but the fish weren't taking that fly yesterday. I used a Parachute Adams fly. Diane used a black gnat."

"What did you use, Porter?"

"Some kind of black fly with a shiny gold wrapping and a little copper bead head. I copied it out of that Colorado Fishing Guide that Paulette bought for me." Porter turned his head and smiled. "Thanks, Paulette."

This comment surprised Paulette. She couldn't remember a time when Porter said, "Thanks," to anyone.

"You are welcome, Porter. We will pick you up for youth group tonight."

"OK."

Some new restaurant guests came in. Paulette hopped up and said a cheery, "Hello," to them. On the white board above the kitchen pass-through was written:

"Take time for friends... they are the source of happiness"

"How did you get started writing books, Mr. Downing?" asked Paulette, refilling Ryan's coffee. I've always wondered how someone can actually sit down and write a book. Want some more orange juice, Porter?"

"No."

"Well," smiled Ryan, "It actually started over an apology. I was selling real estate. The real estate market had slowed down almost to a 'thud.' All of us real estate agents were all having a hard time making sales. I had sold two brand new houses as rentals to an investor client of mine. Ken, another agent in my same office, had also sold five of the new house rentals to investors. All his investors backed out before the closings. Then my investor also backed out. The investors all knew each other. Ken openly blamed Dan, the new home project coordinator, for all of the contract flops. I began blaming Dan, too. Whenever Dan's name came up, I, too, bad-mouthed Dan for my flopped deals."

"One day, I got to feeling very badly. I called up and invited Dan to lunch. We met at the 'Round-The-Corner' hamburger restaurant. I told Dan that I had been 'bad-mouthing' him for about seven months. I told him that I really wasn't that type of person. I just jumped onto Ken's bandwagon and was repeating what Ken had proclaimed. I told him I was sorry and owed him an apology. Dan quietly sat there for a while. Then he said, 'I wondered why you were saying all those things about me.'"

"My words had traveled around and had gotten back to Dan. As Dan and I sat there commiserating about the current bad real estate market, Dan said there were jobs other than real estate."

"Tell me, Ryan;" asked Dan, "If money were no object, and you could have whatever you could choose, what would you like to do if you weren't selling real estate?"

"I don't know of anything I can do."

'Come on, Ryan... name something you have always wanted to do. Everyone has something they would like to do!'

"Dan waited. I sat there thinking. I was in a mental desperation mode because of the slow real estate market. I finally sheepishly spoke up... well... I have always wanted to write a book."

"'Then, write a book!" He demandingly declared.'

"I can't do that!"

"'Why not?'"

"Well, for one thing, I don't know how to type."

"'You can talk, can't you?'"

"I didn't know how to respond."

"'Get yourself a tape recorder and talk into it! We can get someone to transcribe your words later.' Dan was a get-down-to-the-bottom-line-person."

"That's how I got started. I started going up into the mountains on Saturdays every week. I began talking into the tape recorder, pretending that I was speaking to a huge real estate audience. Later, I paid a person from my church to transcribe my words. My first book was about how to use a computer to help sell real estate. Then I wrote some pamphlets, and eventually some short chapters about life, peace, and bible verses."

"So you 'talk' all your books first?" asked Paulette.

"No, that's how I got started. I'm still a two-finger typist. I still don't know how to type."

Porter interjected. "You typed all those books with two fingers and got them published?" It was very unusual for Porter to join into a conversation. Ryan's facial expression and Paulette's eyebrows jumped up almost simultaneously. The outspoken statement surprised both Ryan and Paulette.

Ryan slowly let the words roll out, "Yep...That's just another God-miracle, proof that God can do things any way he wants, using whatever talents a person has."

Porter quickly added, "I see you in your office typing on a new book. Are you typing it with two fingers?"

"Yes, Porter. I am."

"But how did you find out you were a writer? Did God whisper in your ear?" inquired Paulette.

"No. Nothing like that happened. My manuscript was written, but I was afraid to show it to anybody. I put the manuscript in a box in my garage. It stayed there for about nine months. One day, at a 'Salesman with a Purpose' meeting that met every Monday morning, I heard a speaker give a fairly good motivational speech. As a prospecting routine for real estate, if I enjoyed the speaker's talk, I made it a point to go to the speaker's office and try to build a real estate relationship. I went up asked for her business card. That afternoon I stopped by her office. When I was there, I noticed on a shelf, five or six hard-bound books on various topics. Each of the books had her name on them. I asked her how she could be so proficient in that many different areas of knowledge."

"She answered, 'Oh, I don't know anything about all those subjects. I just take what the dry old experts say and make the words flow. I'm a journalist, not an expert.'"

"As our conversation continued, I finally confessed to her that I had written a book. She told me, 'Why don't you bring it by, and I will take a look at it.'"

"I drove home immediately and pulled the manuscript out of the box in the garage. Within forty-five minutes I returned with my printed words. I felt I had to do it right away, because I knew I would get scared and back out if I didn't do it right away. She told me that she would look over the manuscript and get back to me."

Porter joined in suddenly, "Why were you scared?"

"I don't know, Porter. I guess I was afraid of the unknown. I didn't have very much confidence in myself. It was my first book. It took me almost a year before I had the courage to even have someone transcribe my words."

Ryan continued, "She knew how to contact publishers and to secure a contract. She also told me that I had two kinds of books within my writing, a religious book, or a real estate book. She told me to choose between the two. I chose real estate. I asked her what the process was, "write the whole book and then try to find a publisher?"

'Oh no,' she said. 'We write up a couple of sample chapters and submit those. We get a contract first before we do all the work. Do you want me to 'ghost write' the book for you or do you want to be co-authors?"

"I chose co-author. We started meeting at 6:00 AM, twice a week, at her home office. I talked. She typed as I talked. She printed out text for me to review and edit. After we finished the first chapter on real estate sales, she asked me if there was anything unique that I was doing that no other real estate person was doing. I told her that I was the first person in our city to use a computer in my real estate business."

'Computers! That's a hot topic right now. Let's do a chapter on how you use the computer in real estate.'

"Prentice-Hall, a major publisher, took us up on the computer chapter, and gave us a $2,000 advance to get started. Within seven months, the entire hard cover book was written and published."

"That's unbelievable!" chimed in Porter.

"Yes, but it happened for me! By the way, my book didn't sell. The computer revolution sprinted past my book before the ink was dry."

Paulette spoke up, "How did you get started writing your Christian books?"

Ryan continued as if in deep reminiscence... "I just wanted to explain in plain everyday language how faith works in people's lives, that it's not some theoretical journey through life with big unexplainable terminology. I wanted to share with everyone that prayer, faith, and belief are real. Answers to prayers are real. God is real, Jesus is real, and the Bible is real. I wanted to encourage folks with true practical examples. I wanted to share true stories about answers to prayer." Porter was taking in the conversation like a tree root seeking water.

Paulette rubbed her chin, the coffee pot in her hand. "But how did you actually get started? I mean, just how did you begin? Did you use an outline or what?"

"Well, in the Jam, there was another guitar player named Jerry. Occasionally Jerry would bring in some stories he had written which had been published in some magazines. He actually got paid for writing them. His stories were really good. He was a real writer. I asked him one day how he got motivated to write. He laughed, 'Oh, Ryan, you can't wait until you are motivated to write. You wouldn't ever get anything done that way. You just have to go for it.'"

"So...," continued Ryan, "... that's what I do... I turn on my computer and go for it."

"What's the title of your new book that you are working on?" asked Paulette.

"I have a title that I started with... I'm thinking about a new title now. I'm not sure yet."

The conversation lulled for a few moments. Ryan suddenly changed the topic. "Hey, Paulette, this Saturday will be our grand finale gospel jam for the summer. Who all have you invited to the final jam?"

"Everyone is coming, even Mr. Price's ranch staff. They are bringing some of the handicapped kids, too. They can't stay long, but they are still going to bring them by. I put up a poster up on the kitchen wall. Did you see it when you came in? Are you sure a lot of people will be OK to have in your cabin?"

"It will be the highlight of my summer. I think I need to hire you as my Gospel Jam promoter. In Fort Collins, you need to plan to come to the Bluegrass Gospel Jams when you can."

"Diane and I will come, unless we are working. Both of us usually work on Saturdays. It's a busy day for us waitresses."

Turning to Porter, Paulette asked, "Hey, Porter, we will pick you up early today, at 4:45. OK? We are having an outdoor bar-b-q after youth group. Sean and Kristin and the church are bringing the food. We are jamming outside, around a big bonfire. Today is the last youth group meeting. Our youth leaders are leaving for a two-week mission trip to Guatemala. Most all the kids have to go back to school, so this will be our last meeting until next summer."

Ryan read the attractive poster Paulette had created inviting everyone to the Jam on Saturday. Also on the kitchen wall were two new sayings that Paulette had just written a few minutes ago.

"The essence of all health begins with joyful living."

"With wings of faith, you can rise and soar."

# Chapter 25

Porter climbed into the rear seat of the Jeep. Usually sullen and slumped, Porter suddenly sat up straight. Ryan started up the Jeep engine. Out of the blue, Porter began internally admiring the magnificence of the mountain splendor surrounding the two travelers. It was if he had walked into a semi-dark room and had now turned on the light. Porter observed a clarity that he had not seen before. The mountains were "alive with music" a phrase he had remembered from one of Mr. Downing's DVDs, "The Sound of Music."

New thoughts and aspirations began tugging at Porter's mind. Porter did not know what to do with these new revelations and observations. Had he been captured and drawn into a new world by some obsessing demon? He even felt his anger beginning to recede and dissipate. He was loosing grip on something he had held on to for as many years as he could remember. The feeling was unnerving. He had been banished to the "cave in the mountains," for over seven weeks now. He had learned to cook, shop, fish, and eat breakfast out. He started thinking about losing his desire for cigarettes. That feeling had dwindled away, too. These new thoughts encircled his mind. "No TV, no video games. No cell phone. No skateboard. No old friends."

For the very first time, peace had simply and silently enveloped Porter's thoughts. The feeling didn't fit Porter's perception of who he was. Now, who was he? Really?" The question lurking in the back of his mind was, "Why am I sitting in this back seat?"

"When we get back to the cabin, do you want to go and fish the lake?" asked Porter.

Surprised at Porter's question, Ryan glanced up in the rear view mirror, saw Porter's face, and replied, "Sounds great to me... as long as we get back in time for your friends to pick you up tonight. How about I fix supper for a change? I have a desire to whip up some spicy tacos. I will do all the dishes, too. Who do you think will catch the first fish today?"

"Me," replied Porter. "Are there any fish in the river here beside the road?"

"Yes, but the rocky banks make it hard to fish, especially when the runoff is high and rapid. During the low times, almost every pull-off is occupied by city dwellers. I don't like fishing where there are a lot of people all of the time. That's why I feel so fortunate to have a stream and a lake of my own. My rules are simple, 'catch and release.' Are you going to tie some flies to use, Porter?"

"I already have four new ones I tied yesterday. You can use them, too, if you want."

"I think I will!"

There they were, two fishermen, having a conversation about fishing; two fishermen, riding in a jeep.

Substance of the conversation: "Who was going to catch the first fish? Hierarchy of the conversation: unimportant but important. Thrill of victory: residing in Ryan's ears." Porter was actually initiating conversation!

As the Jeep turned off the pavement onto the winding logging road to the cabin, Porter exclaimed, "Look... it's a fox!" Ryan glanced to his right and saw a reddish blur disappear into the bushes. "Yes, you are right, Porter. It's a red fox."

At the cabin, the two fishermen prepared to hike up the trail to the lake. The sun surrounded the cabin with a warm embrace of circling sunshine. Porter fixed the lunch to pack along. He was ready to head up to the lake. "Mr. Downing, I am going to need to use the computer. Can you give me my password?"

"Sure. It's 'PORTer8,' with all capitals except for 'er', which is in lower case. Do you know how to type?"

"Yeah, we had keyboarding in junior high school. I was pretty fast. I enjoyed that class. We learned how to connect to the Internet, too. That was really cool."

"What junior high classes did you enjoy? What were your favorite ones?"

"None, really. I couldn't see any reason for any of my classes. School was just an obstacle I had to endure."

Ryan listened to Porter's response. The phrase, "an obstacle to endure," indicated a flair for using writer's words to express true feelings. Maybe Porter was a better student

193

than what he gave himself credit for. Maybe the potential inside Porter was just under the surface of his angry, unhelpful attitude. Maybe Porter's general non-conversational silence was a cover-up to mask what was tormenting Porter with anger.

"Are you writing your letter to the Judge?"

"Yes," Porter replied with the one word answer. "Let's go fishing. Here are a couple of bead-heads you can try. Ryan accepted the flies and placed them along with his other flies and tucked them into the small white plastic fly box in his fishing vest pocket. Porter led the way at a fairly rapid pace. Ryan trudged behind, going faster than normal. He became winded and often stopped in the shade to catch his breath. Each time, Porter returned and waited for Ryan to start up again. After the third stop, Porter asked, "You OK?"

"Yes. I'm OK. I'm just used to going at my own pace. I'm not used to keeping up with a sprinter youngster like you!"

The old man and the youngster fished the holes of the stream. Soon they both started catching rainbows and brook trout. At Cascade Pool, Porter hooked into a German Brown. The fish broke the surface splashing, and disappeared into the green swirling pool. "I almost got him!" declared Porter.

In "High Mountain Meadow," both fishermen experienced a rapid succession of strikes and "catch and release."

Ryan was celebrating in his mind the fact that both Porter and he were having one of the best fishing afternoons ever. Porter was bounding back and forth across the stream like a bobcat looking for a fish dinner. It took a while but both anglers sat down at the last base of the stream that was pouring out of the lake. The stream at this point was too hard to traverse. The two grinning fishermen sat in the shade and devoured the lunch Porter had prepared. The stream roared as it began its steep descent. The two visitors sat in silence in the majestic stillness. Somehow the stream's roar wasn't the same as traffic rushing by with motors whining.

Old man and teenager sat sipping lemonade on the cabin porch. No conversation emerged. The subdued silence mutually acquiesced between them. Like Ryan's experience of waking up in a hospital after heart surgery, the silence was both deafening and peaceful. The rocking chairs creaked on the wooden porch. Like a ghost, the wind walked by, steadily causing the outstretched yellow flowers to bend with the wind. The tall grasses surrounding the cabin porch also waved gently with the wind. Bird song melodies seemed to merge in mutual unison. Porter was just beginning to sense and hear the birds' songs. He also began noticing that the birds sang both in the day and at night, in the morning, in the evening, now in the afternoon. It was warm. Porter drifted off into sleep, his head resting on his chest and shoulder.

"Tacos are ready!" announced Ryan. Porter jolted up out of the rocking chair, making a squeak on the porch. His neck felt stiff. He had fallen asleep in the rocking chair. He rubbed his neck with his left hand. "Come on in!"

Porter walked into the kitchen and found a fabulous and colorful display of taco fixings. Ryan had prepared a feast. "Help yourself!" Porter began building his super taco with seasoned hamburger, lettuce, chopped tomatoes, diced green onions, yellow shredded cheddar cheese, sour cream, salsa and Mexican Cholula hot sauce. Porter's appetite was hungering and appreciative. Ryan even ate more than normal. Catching fish all morning, hiking, and now feasting together made a special bonding between the old man and the lanky teenager. The peace of the day resided both inside and outside the cabin walls.

Porter spoke up suddenly. "I think I'll go take a shower!" This statement surprised Ryan again. Porter never took a shower during the day. "OK. I got the cleanup taken care of."

Porter and Ryan awaited the arrival of Paulette and friends. Porter pulled out the mandolin and began tuning it. Soon he was picking and strumming parts of melodies of songs. No conversation transpired. The mandolin music melded into the serenity of the mountain setting. Ryan was amazed at the musical skill Porter had developed over such a short period of time. Paulette's Jeep rumbled into the clearing with passengers laughing and joking around. Porter jumped up, put away his mandolin in its case and hurried back into the cabin. He returned with the Bible Sean had given him. He loaded the mandolin case into the back cubbyhole of the Jeep. Porter climbed into his normal seating spot in the back. He put the Bible at his feet. The Jeep rumbled off and disappeared into the trees. The porch was silent, but Ryan could hear the voices of the forest. The bumblebees were droning, the crickets were chirping and the silent stream across the clearing still echoed. He went inside the cabin and watched "Facing the Giants" again.

# Chapter 26

The fellowship hall of the church was packed with jammers and listeners. This was the final main event for the summer youth group bluegrass gospel jams. Within the next week, most of the group would be traveling home. Lively and spirited, the songs quickly evolved spontaneously, in startup unison. Porter was amazed to see person after person come and join in. Some of the jammers, Porter had never seen before. Sean and Kristin kept bringing in more chairs. Everyone was friendly and smiling. Porter felt the urge to smile also.

At the conclusion of the first song, an unfamiliar mandolin player came over and sat in the chair beside Porter. He wore a cowboy hat and had a slender frame. Porter guessed his age to be about 16 or 17. Jeff and Porter slid their chairs outward and sideways to make room. "Hi, my name is Lee. Is this your church?"

Porter stuttered, "No, I have just been here for five or six weeks. I'm going home at the end of this next week."

"Where is home?" asked Lee.

"Florida."

"Have you been playing mandolin for a while?"

"I'm just a beginner."

"When I heard about this jam," said Lee, "a few of my friends and I decided to come up and join in. We all live about ten miles up the canyon. We have a small get-together too. We usually have four or five. Too bad this is the last jam for the summer."

Somebody hollered out, "Let's do, 'I'll Fly Away' in G."

In unison, the players all picked up the tempo. Porter could play this song. It was the first song he had learned. Now, sitting near two mandolin players, a surge of energy gave Porter more confidence than ever before. He could actually keep up with the rest of the musicians! All in all, there were about fourteen musicians, including 2 banjos, 2 fiddle players, 2 guitar players, autoharp player, stand up bass player, 3 mandolin players, a harmonica player, and a keyboard player. Another musician entered with a washboard around her neck. She had come in with wooden spoons in one hand...

There were about twenty people in the audience. The room bulged with music. Musicians and audience were all participating in song. "How could they know that many songs?" thought Porter.

Sean and Kristin were leading the song selections, choosing and guiding musicians to make their choices. They also started inviting requests from the audience. Sean & Kristin led most of the songs in G, C, and D. Jeff showed Porter how to change chords on the right words. All of a sudden, Porter could keep up with Jeff. Porter shoved his chair forward slightly so he could see Jeff's finger positions. Porter began hearing the chord changes in his mind. He was definitely clumsy, but his persistence made Porter feel like a real musician. In short, Porter was having a good time.

Hayden Price appeared at the doorway of the jamming room. "Got room for another banjo player?" Several musicians slid over, making room for the new joiner. Immediately the jam group started playing, "Unclouded Day." Mr. Price joined right in with a thumping banjo beat. Porter tried to keep up.

After the group progressed through about twenty song selections, Sean stood up and announced to the musicians and audience. "It's so great to have you all come tonight to our youth group gospel jam. We have been holding the jam every Wednesday night through the summer. At each jam, we always give every person in our group the opportunity to share a Bible verse that has helped them during the week. We would like to take a few minutes before the snack break to give our youth that opportunity again. Does anyone have a verse to share?"

There was a pregnant silence. Jeff suddenly stood up with his mandolin in his hand. Porter was amazed. "Yes, I have a verse..." Everyone's eyes focused on Jeff. "I was sent up to Mr. Price's ranch by a court order. Back where I live, some friends of mine, and I, trashed out the school where I was attending. We vandalized the whole school. I think we were mad at some teachers, who tried to discipline us. There was no true reason for our actions, but I was sent here to earn enough money to pay back some of the damage costs. Working with handicapped kids has given me a fresh introspection on life. Playing in this jam has also helped my new outlook. I'm sorry for what I did." Jeff found his marked Bible passage. "I found this verse in the Bible that's beginning to make sense to me:

Galatians 5: 22

"But the fruit of the Sprit is love, joy, peace, patience, kindness, goodness, faithfulness, gentleness, and self-control." Jeff sat down slowly.

The group gathering was hushed.

Suddenly, Porter stood up. With voice shaking, but energized by Jeff's admission, he started in on his story. "At the beginning of this past year, I was 15. A friend of mine was 16. He had just received his driving license. He was a wild kid, always stirring up something. I went along with him on all his ventures into getting into trouble. One Saturday morning this year, he let me drive his car. I didn't know how to drive, but he urged me to go ahead, anyway. After a few blocks, I drove right through a red light. A policeman was there on the corner. He pulled us over with red light flashing. He found out that I was driving without a license, under age, and totally irresponsible with my attitude. He gave me a ticket and ticketed my friend. 'You guys will have to show up in court in two weeks.'"

"My friend and I spent the rest of the day just goofing off, daring other cars to drag race. Around 5:00 that afternoon, my friend found someone to race. The residential street was separated by a median of bushes and trees. There were 2 lanes on each side. The drag race was on. I encouraged my friend to go faster and faster. I was on an emotional high. Then suddenly, I heard a scream and a thump. We stopped as soon as we could. The other racer kept right on going. We saw the six-year girl in the street, head bleeding... and dead."

Porter paused. "When the police officer came up to investigate the accident, it was the same policeman who had given us the tickets earlier that morning. I have lived with that scream and thump ever since it happened. No, I wasn't the driver... but I feel guilty as hell. Anyway, that's why the Judge gave the order to have me ride in the back seat, as a reminder. I don't have a Bible verse to share because I'm not up on this Bible stuff. All I know is that God must be watching out over me, even though he has no reason to do so. I now appreciate Mr. Price's camp, this bluegrass gospel youth group, and especially, Mr. Downing, for allowing me to stay up here these past two months at my Grandpa Quentin's cabin. By court order, I have to write letters to the Judge and Mr. Downing. I don't know if it's right or not, when I get back home, I'm going to write a letter to that girl's parents."

Porter sat down, his whole frame shaking and sobbing. Sean announced, "Let's do, 'Amazing Grace' for both Jeff and Porter." The voices rang out in acapella unison with the words of the song. "I was blind, but now I see!"

202

The room was as silent as the woods at night. Sean bowed his head and prayed, "Lord we come to you in awesome wonder on what you have done to help transform the individual lives of these two boys who have just opened their hearts to us and to you. Please send the right companions for Jeff and Porter. Help them trust in you. Help them become ambassadors for you and your love. Thank you. Amen!"

"Let's eat!" chimed in Kristin.

All the kids came over and congratulated Jeff and Porter, shaking their hands and clapping them on their backs. "That took a lot of courage, Porter," said someone.

Porter was amazed that the youth group teens he didn't know came over and shook his hand. Both Jeff and Porter were overwhelmed by the instant cheerful encouraging responses. "I'll pray for you." "We will be praying for you." After the snacks, the jam resumed with a lively chorus of fast moving bluegrass lyrics. Sean was asked why the jams were called, Bluegrass Gospel Jams.

"These are down-home songs primarily based on Bible Verses. We are preserving part of our parent's and grandparents' heritage. Music is just one way God communicates with us. Maybe... and this is what I believe... this is a way for us to communicate with God. I believe God invented and inspired music. Music is another way of reaching people, when words cannot do it alone. And, it proves that Christians can have fun, too."

As the Jam concluded, Mr. Price came over to Jeff and Porter. "I'm very proud of you Jeff... you too, Porter. "Maybe you two could figure out a way to come up to the ranch this next summer. We can always use good help!"

The trip back down the canyon was lively and spirited. All of Porter's companions gave him the front passenger seat. Porter's life was beginning to take a turn for the better. As they dropped off Jeff, Porter grabbed his arm, "Thanks, man. You were very brave! I appreciate it." Porter suddenly wondered why he had never said words of appreciation before... to anybody.

The trip through the trees back to Mr. Downing's cabin was pitch-black. Paulette's Jeep crawled through the trees with only the headlights piercing the darkness. A white and gray fog had enveloped both the cabin and surrounding forest. Porter had returned later than usual. Paulette spoke as Porter climbed out of the front seat, "It's too bad the summer is already over. Thanks for opening up with your feelings, Porter. I will pray for you... our whole youth group will be praying for you. Maybe we will meet again somewhere." As the Jeep exited into the foggy darkness, Porter stood there, his thoughts churning.

Porter sat in one of the rocking chairs on the porch. The evening was balmy and white with fog. He could tell Mr. Downing had already turned in. The glow from the fireplace was visible from the porch. An unusual calmness settled in. This was a new emotional experience for Porter. He felt a sense of relief that he had never experienced before. His pent-up anger emotions began settling out of his mind. Porter breathed in a deep breath of the foggy mountain air. He sat in the rocking chair for over an hour, staring out at the white darkness. He had a sense of loneliness but the cabin setting made him feel like he wasn't alone. He felt strangely comfortable and welcomed by the screened-in cabin porch. He went inside the kitchen and picked out a can of cold Sprite from the refrigerator. He took an apple from the fruit bowl. He returned to the rocking chair. The fog slowly began lifting, showing the outlines of the pine trees, now illuminated by the pale moonlight. The wind stilled as the fog lifted its grip upon the forest. Stars started appearing. Porter stayed out on the porch, thinking, and finally went to bed about 2:15 AM.

# Chapter 27

Ryan awoke to the sound of chattering squirrels and singing sparrows. The forest was coming alive with the rosy dawning of the day. He showered and shaved, taking his time. He thought about cooking breakfast in the cabin. Then he decided, "Nope, I'm going out to breakfast!" Ryan went to Porter's bedroom and hollered out to him, "Hey Porter, want to go to breakfast?" He repeated his question twice more. Porter didn't budge. He was asleep again like a log on the forest floor. Ryan went into the kitchen and wrote a note for Porter, telling him that he had gone down to Mountain Greenery. He placed the time on the note, 7:45 AM.

The short twenty-minute drive to the restaurant invigorated Ryan. The yellow-gold sun warmed the mountain air. The air was refreshing and invigorating. He always got a thrill out of driving through these mountain majesties. He had a bluegrass gospel CD playing. He felt close to God. He silently thanked God for providing this majestic splendor displayed before him. In his whole being, Ryan was experiencing peace. The music, the sun, the air, and the everlasting mountain beauty gave Ryan inspiration. In his mind, he started planning another trip up to the lake when he returned from breakfast. There was still a spot where a big German Brown trout was still lurking...up past that rock that jutted into the lake. "Maybe Porter will want to go. He's been getting more interested in fishing here lately."

Ryan pulled into the long gravel parking lot beside the restaurant. SUVs and pickups were already there. He walked in the screen door, jingling the small bell on top of the door. All the patrons said hello to Ryan. He acknowledged the friendly greetings and went over to his favorite booth by the window. Soon, Paulette came by with ice water and hot steaming coffee. "Want your usual?" inquired Paulette.

"You know what? I'd like to change and try something different this morning. How about bringing me the Breakfast Burrito? It sure looks good when I see other people order it."

"Sure! Would you like some juice to go with it?"

"Yes, orange juice, large...and coffee."

"It might take a little longer this morning. Everyone here ordered a huge meal this morning. I guess they all got hungry on the same morning at the same time.

"No problem! I'm in no great hurry. All I have to do is to go fishing later today."

"When will your new book be finished?" asked Paulette.

"Probably by the end of this summer... I only write when I feel motivated. Actually, that's not entirely true. When I set a day or time in my mind, I just start writing, whether I'm motivated or not. Today my mind is focused on fishing. It's too nice to sit behind a computer all day."

"What's the title of your book going to be?"

"Log Cabin Miracles," replied Ryan.

"Order pickup," echoed a voice from the kitchen.

Paulette hurried over to the kitchen. Ryan sipped the curly steaming hot coffee. The door bell tinkled as Hayden Price walked in. He had to stoop so his cowboy hat wouldn't get knocked off. He spotted Ryan and sauntered over to Ryan's booth. "Mind if I join you, Ryan?"

"Not at all... welcome. Have a seat. You are up and about early. I thought you had to stick around the ranch in the mornings to keep things going."

"Well, it's the end of our season. Everything is winding down now, so I don't have as much to do. Have you ordered, yet?"

"I just did... but there are a lot of orders ahead of me. You can order and we could have our breakfast together, I think your order would be the next one after mine. I just now ordered. Look, here comes Paulette."

"Hi, Mr. Price... you are up early today. Can I get you some coffee? Do you want to order breakfast?"

"Yes...coffee... and water. I would like to order breakfast, too."

"We are running a little behind, today."

"That's OK."

"What would you like?"

Mr. Price pushed back the brim of his cowboy hat. "I think I'll have the Farmer's Son Breakfast, scrambled eggs, bacon, and sourdough toast."

"That's what I usually order," said Ryan. "Today, I changed my mind and just for kicks. I ordered a breakfast burrito."

"Where is Porter? asked Hayden, "I thought you two always ate breakfast out together."

"Yes, we usually do. But this morning he was dead asleep. I couldn't get him to wake up. That's unusual because he has been a very light sleeper lately. He must have gotten home late last night. I turned in early and didn't hear him come in."

Hayden pulled out a folded paper from his coat pocket. "I thought I would find Porter here. Could I ask you to do a favor for me? Give this application to Porter. Have him fill it out and get it back to me."

Ryan took the paper and looked at the title. "Why are you giving Porter an application?"

"I would like to have Porter work for me next year... if he can figure out a way to get here. I know Tampa, Florida, is a long way to come. I'm hoping Porter can save enough money over the next year. He told me he wants to get a job after school every day. He wants to work weekends, too. Maybe this application will help him set a goal. He's good with the handicapped kids. I gave an application to Jeff, too. It's amazing how those two developed such a neat friendship in such a short time. The job would be full time and both boys would receive meals and lodging. Jeff loves being around the horses. Both boys love playing the mandolin. They both like going to the summer youth group bluegrass gospel jams up at the church. You should have more gospel jams at your cabin... The whole youth group is always talking about the good jamming times we had at Mr. Downing's Jam."

"Maybe next summer we can plan on some more gospel jams," replied Ryan. "I'm just about finished with my most recent book. My book writing time has been a little sparse since Porter came up. I already have some speaking engagements lined up for the middle and end of September."

"What do you speak about?" asked Hayden.

"Peace, well my first four books were about, 'The Pursuit of Peace.' These were Christian books based on the Bible and my own personal faith victories." So I became known as, 'The Peace Man.'"

"So are you still known as 'The Peace Man'?"

"Yes, but I now have a new title, 'Bluegrass Gospel Jam Ambassador'"

Paulette returned, steadying both breakfast meals on her arms. I thought you two would enjoy having your breakfasts come out at the same time. She placed the plates in front of Mr. Price and Ryan. "I'll get you both some more coffee. I'll be right back." Ryan paused, "Hayden, I usually say a prayer before a meal, if it's OK with you."

"So do I. Go ahead." The two men bowed their heads and Ryan spoke. "Dear Lord, thank you for this time where we can acknowledge you for always being with us. We ask you bless this meal for your good works that you accomplish through us. Thank you. Amen!"

Paulette refilled the coffee cups. "Where is Porter today?"

"Asleep. I couldn't wake him this morning."

Paulette responded, "He was probably getting his first restful sleep that he has had in a long time."

"What do you mean?" asked Mr. Downing.

"Well... he opened up at the gospel jam and shared ... with everyone... some of the stuff that's been bothering him. So did Jeff... Jeff went first. I think Jeff's story inspired Porter."

"I don't understand..." said Mr. Downing, "Porter has never shown or shared his feelings with anyone, at least not me. I've noticed some positive changes recently... with his attitude."

"Didn't Porter tell you what happened last night at youth group?" said Paulette.

"No, I haven't talked to him."

Hayden interjected, "Yes, it was a total surprise coming from both Jeff and Porter. Sean gave the kids an invitation to share a Bible verse. Jeff shared with the group why he had been sent to my ranch. Afterwards, Porter stood up and shared his story. Both young men opened up their souls during that gospel jam. The response from the group was overwhelmingly supportive. Sean opened the door for two young musicians to join in. I had tears in my eyes, too."

Paulette said, "Yes, Porter explained about the accident that killed that 6-year old girl. It wasn't entirely his fault, but the accident really affected him. We found out why he had the restriction of always riding in the back seat. On the way back, we all urged him to sit in the front seat. It was our way of supporting his sharing and the opening up his heart. We had the best jam, ever. We played far into the night. The whole youth group is praying for both Jeff and Porter. We have been praying for them all along. I guess God does answer prayers in mysterious ways... You guys better eat your breakfasts before they get cold." Paulette left and began refilling the other patrons' coffee mugs.

Hayden continued, "I wanted to give some encouragement to Jeff and Porter. That's why I decided to invite them both to work for me, next summer," said Hayden. "Sean and the gospel jam helped both of these boys. I even think the judges that sent them to you and me had caring hearts, too. I wouldn't be surprised if both judges are Christians."

Ryan replied, "This a real victory story for me. I have been praying, too. When I took on the task of helping a troubled teenager, I was completely out of my element. I had no confidence or knowledge of what to do. So I prayed a lot. I agree with you. Now I see again... what God can do when we pray. God sent these two boys to us so he could work his way with the boys. Now, I have another true story to include in my book. Prayer truly does work wonders."

"I agree," said Hayden... "Wholeheartedly."

The saying on the kitchen wall stated, "Better to do something imperfectly than to do nothing flawlessly." Robert H. Schuler, author and pastor.

"Hey Mr. Downing...can Diane and I come up fishing this next week, before we have to go back to school?

# Chapter 28

Ryan's spirits were high as he guided his Jeep back to the cabin. He turned up the CD player. "My Old Friend", started in with banjo and "I am Thine O Lord." This was a CD by Mount Zion, recorded by one of his bluegrass gospel jam musician contacts. This was down-home inspiration. He opened both front windows and let the wind blow through. He felt like a teenager again from years past. He guided the Jeep into the cabin clearing. Porter was sitting on one of the rocking chairs on the porch. He was reading a book.

"Hi,"

Ryan was taken aback some. This was the first time Porter had ever said a greeting first. He returned the greeting, "Hi Porter."

"I tried to wake you this morning to go to breakfast but you were really sound asleep."

"That's OK. I fixed myself some bacon and eggs and toast. Don't worry... I cleaned up the kitchen and washed all the dishes." Porter gazed ahead towards the open clearing. "I saw a big bull moose come through the clearing. I was just sitting here reading... when I heard a soft snorting sound. He just ambled across the edge of the clearing and back into the woods and disappeared. I should have tried to take a picture but I didn't want to move and scare him off."

Ryan replied, "I have seen lots of deer and a few elk, but I have never seen a moose here before. You should count that sighting as an achievement. I don't think there are any moose back in Florida, are there? What book are you reading?"

"It's the Living Bible. Sean, from the youth group, gave it to me. Mr. Downing, can you tell me again what my password is to get into the Word program. I need to write my letters. Are you writing your book today?"

"Your password is 'PORTer'. No I'm not writing today. You can use the computer. I'm going up to the lake and sit on the bank and enjoy this nice warm weather. You can come along, if you want."

"No, I'll stay here," answered Porter.

Ryan thought about asking Porter about what happened at youth group last night, but he decided to wait until Porter was open to discussing it. As he put on his fishing gear, he placed the application that Hayden had given him, on the kitchen breakfast bar. He packed a Jonathan apple, 2 granola bars, 2 bottles of water, an orange, some cashew nuts, and made a double-slice ham sandwich with yellow and gray-flecked  horseradish mustard. The zip lock bags were perfect for transporting food. He placed his "never-worn-yet" baseball cap on his head which read, "Fishing Cheaper Than Therapy."

"I'm headed up to the lake. See you later this afternoon."

"OK," replied Porter.

"Ryan chose a steady leisurely pace, resting every 15 minutes so he wouldn't get out of breath. Some years back, he had a double by-pass heart operation. At the beginning of this year, his cardiologist doctor told Ryan that he only had one-third of his heart capacity to work with. His enlarged heart was simply pumping too fast, making him out of breath under any kind of rapid exertion. Ryan came up to the cabin to establish, maintain, and cultivate peace. He could sit by a stream, or a lake, in the sun, even without a fishing pole, and still be energized by the mountains and nature surrounding him. A warm breeze picked up with short gusts of warm air. The air currents swirled around, picking up dead leaves.

Ryan sat down on a mound of tufted weeds and consumed a granola bar. He downed half of a bottle of distilled water. He glanced over his shoulder. There sat beneath a shady tree, a plump cottontail rabbit, chewing on long, green grasses. The rabbit seemed to not notice that a human was there. Ryan watched the rabbit for five minutes before the rabbit ambled along. Ryan pondered on what that rabbit might be thinking.

After the series of short rests, after a short steep climb, Ryan finally appeared at the rim of the natural mountain lake. The water was sky blue, reflecting the white clouds that were drifting by. This was unusual for the lake to be calmly still. Most of the time there was always a breeze of some kind. Two black crows winged overhead, perching in the tops of the trees on the other side of the lake. Higher up, an eagle was circling and soaring leisurely, seemingly unaware of anything happening below. Ryan perched himself up beside the huge boulder that jutted into the lake.

He unfolded his fishing chair. He began his methodical casting pattern. He sent the water-filled bobber flying out into the darker portion of the lake. Tied three feet behind, the large black Wooly Bugger floated partly submerged, about four inches below the water surface. He reeled in steadily, waiting for that small sometimes strong tug. It seemed that when a fish took a fly, the fish was already on the run. He patiently kept on casting for about 45 minutes. The sun started climbing. A soft breeze started rippling across the placid lake. The bobber started dancing up and down as he reeled in. Then Ryan felt a sudden large tug. The line shot out straight. The fish was on! He instinctively pulled up on his casting rod. The drag on his reel "whirred," as the line shot out and away from Ryan. He had a big one! "This fish is going anywhere he wants!" The drag whirred again as the fish took off in different directions. The huge fish jumped out of the water probably eight to ten times. Ryan checked to see if he had his fishing net. He didn't. He was now standing a few feet away from the rock, standing in the lake shallows, playing the grand fish with all the skill he had. Several times, the fish rolled just under the surface. The fish was jumping like a Rainbow Trout. "It must be a German Brown!"

The contest lasted for about 20 minutes until the fish began tiring. Ryan finally was able to drag the enormous fish up onto the sandy bank. Ryan measured the great fish. It was 23 inches long and must have weighed five pounds. The Wooly Bugger fly was lodged in the fish's upper jaw. He took the digital camera from his fishing vest pouch and snapped 4 pictures. He immediately placed the extra long trout back into the shallow water, his gills flapping. The trout lay on its side, then straightened upright and weaved his way back into the lake. The day was already a success, both for fisherman and fish.

Ryan fished for another hour, with no strikes. He decided to have lunch. He sat in the warm sun shining down and reflecting off the boulder. He ate his sandwich and some of the snacks. As he sipped his water, he spied movement on the left side of the lake. Three deer emerged on the bank and took a drink out of the lake. "That's unusual," he thought. "Deer don't usually show up during the day, except for mornings and evenings. Maybe that's because we never look for deer during the day. I wonder how many other critters are out there. Pauline said she saw a bobcat the other day, down by the river. I sure have seen a lot of deer this summer."

Rested and full, Ryan stayed at his same spot. The thrill of catching such a huge fish still lingered. As soon as he threw in his line, on his first cast, a rainbow trout leaped out of the water. Ryan pulled and hooked him. He was a medium sized fish with sparkling red gills. The fish leaped out of the water three different times. When he returned the fish to the water, the brightly striped trout shot out into the depths of the lake. Ryan fished all afternoon in the heat of the day. Fish kept biting, fighting, and escaping. For some unknown reason, this was the best fishing day ever. There was fishing action all the rest of the afternoon.

The sky clouded. The wind picked up its gusts. It was time for the daily afternoon mountain shower, Ryan never wore a watch. He guessed the time to be around 3:15. The wind was cooling. He decided to head back down the trail. He looked up at the sky. Up high the weather had been shining and hot. Now on the way down, the sky was turning dark and black. Soon, thunder rolled and lightning crackled. Now the trail was being covered by a cover of white bubbly hailstones. He pulled on his waterproof windbreaker. He stopped and got underneath the sprawling branches of a large blue spruce tree. It was dry here. As if it were a stream, the trail started flowing water. The thunderstorm lasted for about 15 minutes. Then the sun came out again. Curls of steam vaporized upward as the day returned to its normal sunny self. As Ryan neared the cabin clearing, he could smell the odor of charcoal burning. Porter was pouring more coals on top of the already smoldering coals.

"Catch any?" called out Porter.

"Yep! It was the best fishing day I have ever had! I caught the biggest fish I have ever caught!" Ryan went into great detail about his grand fishing day.

Porter listened intently. "I finished writing my letters today," announced Porter, suddenly. "I thought we would have dinner on the porch tonight. I'm fixing those two sirloin steaks I bought last week. I found a recipe for scalloped onions, carrots, and French green beans, in that Guideposts magazine. Right now, I have the steaks marinating in some bar-b-q sauce with some lemon pepper, garlic powder, and steak sauce. I'm also baking some potatoes wrapped in foil in the coals. We have butter and sour cream in the refrigerator. I was just making sure the grill was hot enough. I didn't know when you would be back.

Ryan again marveled at the conversation flowing from this usually sullen, one-sentence teenager. He was also amazed that Porter had taken on his own initiative, the task of preparing supper. "When did you put the potatoes in?

"About a half hour ago," replied Porter.

"Let them bake about 30 minutes more. You can tell when they are done by sticking a fork into them."

"I also made some butterscotch pudding for dessert. It's in the fridge. I just followed the directions on the box."

"Sounds like a celebration feast, Porter, both for you, and for me. Can I do anything to help?"

"You can finish setting the table, if you want. I have a question, why did you put that application to Mr. Price's ranch on the kitchen table?

"Mr. Price wants you to work for him this next summer. He met me for breakfast to hand it to you personally, but you weren't there. He asked me if I would get it to you. We had a nice breakfast conversation. He said that he thought you had potential. It just has to be developed. He gave an application to Jeff, too. He said both you boys were very good with the handicapped kids. He said he could always use good help. The job sounds pretty good. You get all your meals and lodging included for the three summer months. All you have to do is to raise and save enough money to get there. He told me that you were planning on getting a part-time job after school. This could be a great goal for you. I think Mr. Price is the kind of person who wants to help troubled teenagers find a passion."

"Passion?" inquired Porter. "What's passion?"

"Passion is something that develops over time when you begin discovering what you want your life to look like. Instead of being angry and soured at the world, you start spending your energies on something worthwhile, that you enjoy doing. Life can be a lot simpler and happier when you get rid of anger and start forgiving people for their imperfections. Mr. Price sees the opportunity to help you find a purpose for your life. You should be mighty thankful that there are a lot of people who care about you. I need to go in and wash this fish smell off my hands."

"Potatoes are done," announced Porter. "The steaks are just about done."

Teenager and old man sat around the "victory feast." The atmosphere was jovial. The "William Tell Overture" playing on the CD player flooded the cabin with enthusiasm and excitement. "How can I get this application back to Mr. Price?" asked Porter.

"Have you already filled it out?" asked Ryan.

"I filled it out this afternoon..."

"We could go to breakfast in the morning and ask Paulette to give it to Mr. Price. Paulette said he usually comes in every day in the early afternoon."

"OK."

"Paulette and Diane are coming up tomorrow after lunch to fish the lake. Maybe you would like to go along."

"Wouldn't you want to go fishing again at the same spot?"

"I would," Ryan replied, "but I have some work I want to do on the computer. You kids go ahead. Your dad is picking you up this Saturday. So you better get as much fishing in as you can. This is a beautiful time of the year..."

"Here is your letter," said Porter, handing Ryan a sealed envelope with "Mr. Downing" written on the outside. "Let's have our pudding out on the porch. We can go to breakfast in the morning."

Ryan and Porter sat on the porch. The forest was quiet. Stars started appearing. The moon was slowly rising. Neither of the forest visitors spoke. Silence enveloped the cabin and the clearing. The two rocking chairs creaked in unison, like two crickets. The Coleman lantern on the center table glowed, sending off effervescent rays into the starry, black void.

# Chapter 29

Porter and Mr. Downing arrived at the restaurant about 8:30. The restaurant was already packed. Porter chose the last booth by the windows. The message board on the kitchen wall displayed:

"Keep on loving each others as brothers. Do not forget to entertain strangers, for by so doing some people have entertained angels without knowing it." Hebrews 13: 1-2

Paulette greeted them warmly. She brought water and coffee for Ryan. "Hi, Mr. Downing... hi, Porter... What will you gentlemen have today? Your usual order for breakfast?"

"Yes," replied Mr. Downing.

"OK," replied Porter.

"I get off right after lunch today" said Paulette. Diane is coming up, too. We are coming up to go fish that lake of yours, Mr. Downing. Do you want to hike up to the lake with us, Porter? I know that you have to go back this Saturday. Diane and I will be going back on Monday."

"Yes, I would," stated Porter. Porter's positive response surprised both Paulette and Mr. Downing.

"I will put your order in."

The doorbell had a little ring. Hayden Price ducked into the restaurant. He came over to Ryan and Porter's table. "I was just heading into town and I saw your Jeep. I figured Porter would be here too."

Paulette came over quickly, "Do you want to order some breakfast, Mr. Price?"

"No, just coffee, thanks." Mr. Price sat down beside Ryan. "Hi, Porter. Going back soon I hear. Saturday?"

"Yes." Porter reached inside his jacket and pulled out the envelope with the ranch application. He slid the envelope over to Mr. Price.

"Is it filled out?

"Yes."

"Do you think you can find a way to return here next summer?"

Paulette came over with Mr. Price's coffee.

"I think so. I'm going to try to get a job after school and save some money. Is Jeff coming back, too?"

"Yes, he told me the same thing. I think you two boys can work together real well."

Mr. Price finished his coffee. "Well... gotta' go into town. See you later."

"I got your coffee, Hayden."

"Thanks. See you later."

Paulette came over with the coffee pot as Mr. Price was leaving. "Only one cup of coffee today, Mr. Price?"

"I have to go in town to the feed store. The horses are getting hungry again." Mr. Price tipped his hat and left.

Paulette filled Ryan's coffee cup. She turned to Porter, "I heard you and Jeff got invited back to Mr. Price's ranch next summer. Jeff said you were going to try to make it back."

"Yeah, replied Porter, "I'm going to try. I have to see what the Judge says when I get back. I sure wish I could just erase part of my life, especially that one day."

"Porter, it really took a lot of courage for you to open up to the youth group the other night. I'm sure you helped others in the group."

"Me?" questioned Porter. "How could what I said help someone else?"

"Each of us has some problems of our own," replied Paulette. "We aren't perfect just because we are in a youth group or we believe in God. You never know, you may have influenced someone you don't even know. Either way, it's important to confess and start over. You can live a much better life from this point on. I think God sent you here on purpose. He will allow you to start over. He forgives... without judgment."

"I never had good friends, people who cared about me. I always chose the down-and-outers who just got me into trouble. I think I was a big pain in the neck for my Mom. I'm going to try changing that when I get back."

"Porter, the whole youth group is praying for you. If you keep talking to God, he can help you find your path. God loves you! Diane and I will be praying for you, too." Porter didn't know what to say.

Mr. Downing engaged conversation with Porter, who suddenly became very talkative. In Mr. Downing's eyes, the conversation was "normal". Questions were mutually asked and answered from both teenager, and old man. They remained at the restaurant for another hour and a half. "See you soon," said Mr. Downing, as he paid the ticket. I think you, Diane, and Porter are going to have a grand fishing day! I sure had my grand day yesterday!"

Mr. Downing and Porter cruised down the canyon. Now that the spring runoff had dwindled, the stream flowed more leisurely. The jeep rumbled as they bounced up towards the cabin.

"Sounds like you have made some good friends, Porter."

# Chapter 30

After Porter, Diane, and Paulette began the trek up to the lake, Ryan opened the envelope Porter had given him yesterday. The letter was short.

Dear Mr. Downing,

Thank you for letting me stays with you here at your cabin for these past 2 months. I thought I was being punished by the Judge and my Dad by sending me here. Instead, I received a glimmer of hope for my life. I appreciate the opportunities you gave me to accept responsibilities. I learned to cook, fish, and how to go to breakfast. I even learned some play-along songs on the mandolin. The youth group at church took me in, even when they discovered what I was like back home in Florida. They had no reason to, but they did. Thanks again for putting up with me. I know I was a pain in the butt. I want to change. I would like to be the first one to read your book you are writing. Oh, another thing, I've enjoyed the peace I have experienced here.

Your friend, Porter.

Ryan sealed up the letter into another envelope. He began his letter to Judge Brown.

Dear Judge Brown,

Porter has lived with me for almost two months now. I must admit that I wasn't too sure of what I was in for, when

I agreed to take him in. I was not youthfully enthusiastic about learning to understand a troubled teenager. It was very difficult for an old man and a 15 year old teenager to handle the awkward situations. I have done a lot of praying for Porter. His attitude has improved 300%.

I see potential in Porter. I think, if he surrounds himself with solid Christian friends, that he will become a better person in society. He has had a glimpse of a more positive side of life. I think he actually wants to continue hanging out with better friends. I don't believe he wants to go back to his old way of life. If his mother would restrain herself from continually yelling at Porter, Porter can probably become more like his dad. Porter learned to know what it is like to help out handicapped kids. He learned to become an encourager. Hayden Price operates a guest ranch for handicapped kids. Mr. Price has offered Porter a full time job this next summer. Porter actually filled out the job application and gave it to Mr. Price, all on his own.

Porter has been attending a church youth group and playing the mandolin in a bluegrass gospel jam. He opened up and openly shared with the kids and leader of the youth group. He is sorry for what his actions have been. I'm not a counselor so I don't know what to tell you. I just have this feeling that Porter should be given another chance. I don't think going to jail will help Porter. He needs encouragement and accountability, for sure. I believe he has made a course correction in his mind and spirit. I would like to see how that course correction can produce positive results.

My recommendation is that we bypass the jail sentence. I feel everyone should take a chance with Porter and monitor and see what happens. As you requested I have included Porter's thank you letter to me.

Sincerely, Ryan Downing

P.S. I am including Porter's letter to you without opening it. I believe that letter is between Judge and teenager.

Mr. Downing placed all 3 sealed letters in a large envelope and addressed it to Judge Brown. "I'll mail this tomorrow."

Old man and teenager entered the restaurant, first ones there. Paulette greeted them warmly. "Sit where you like."

The message above the kitchen was:

Psalm 121:1-2

"I lift up my eyes to the hills- where does my help come from? My help comes from the Lord, the Maker of heaven and earth."

"You are becoming much bolder with your daily messages, Paulette," said Mr. Downing.

"You know," replied Paulette, "those verses seem to inspire people's spirits. Most of the customers never mind. I'm happy Sharon has encouraged and allowed me to post my messages. What will you two have for breakfast? Your usual? I hear you are leaving the canyon tomorrow, Porter. How about something different, like our corned beef hash and eggs and butter croissant special?"

"That sounds great to me," offered Porter.

"Me, too," agreed Mr. Downing.

"I'll bring your coffee and orange juice." Paulette returned with the drinks.

"You ready to go back tomorrow, Porter?"

"No. Believe it or not, I'm just now settling in. I'm not looking forward to returning to the city. I like it here. But I have to go. I have no other choice."

"Maybe you can find a good youth group at a church. Maybe you can seek out and find a bluegrass gospel jam."

Paulette returned with two steaming piles of corned beef hash. "Hey Porter, Sean called me a few minutes ago. I was supposed to ask you if you would like to come up to a youth group picnic this afternoon? It's kind of an end of season spur-of-the-moment going-away party for everyone. The church is furnishing all the food. We are planning on playing some music, too."

"I have to go into town and meet with Nathan this afternoon." said Mr. Downing.

"Paulette, can you come and pick up Porter?"

"Better than that," replied Paulette, "I get off around 11:00 today. Porter can stay here at the restaurant, and we can go from here, if that's OK with you, Porter."

Almost embarrassedly, Porter responded with, "Yeah... OK."

Porter and Mr. Downing bowed their heads. "Would you like to say the prayer, Porter?" asked Mr. Downing.

"I don't know how."

"Just say, thanks, Lord"

Porter stiffened, bowed his head, and replied in a strong vibrant tone. "Thank you Lord, for this breakfast, my friends, and well... everything. Amen." Paulette listened to Porter's prayer as she came over and refilled Mr. Downing's coffee mug.

"Diane is coming up around 10:00, Porter. You two can talk out on the patio. It's going to be a hot, terrific day. We will bring Porter home after the picnic." Mr. Downing left Porter at the restaurant and headed down the canyon.

Ryan met for coffee with Nathan. Their conversation lasted for over one and a half hours. Nathan was in a glib mood. His real estate sales had picked up momentum. He had two closings happening later that day.

"When things slow down, Nathan, why don't you come up this next week and go fishing? Take a day off. I will prepare all the food. Porter and I have pretty much cleaned out the cabinets and refrigerator I'm going to the grocery store later this morning and stock up on groceries. What kind of lunch and supper do you want?"

"Did you say Porter is going back to Florida, tomorrow? When is he leaving? Did you get things to work out?"

"Porter's dad is coming sometime tomorrow afternoon. He emailed me this morning. Porter has to meet with the Judge when he gets back. I think Porter would rather stay another month. He really started coming around these past few weeks."

"The peace and serenity got to him, huh?"

"I think so... and good friends his own age. He started going to a youth group at a church up there. He even started playing the mandolin in some bluegrass gospel jams. He also helped out once a week at a ranch for handicapped kids. Anyway, Nathan, the cabin will be quiet, all except for the forest sounds, and the rushing streams. All I'm doing there these next two weeks is finishing up my latest book... and fishing... Wait until I tell you about German Brown Rock..."

Ryan stopped by the post office, purchased postage, and mailed Judge Brown's bulging envelope.

# Chapter 31

Porter awoke to the sounds of birds singing and squirrels chattering. The wind outside seemed to carry the sound of rushing stream water. He heard "clinking" coming from the kitchen. Rousing banjo tunes filled the cabin. Porter pulled on his jeans and tennis shoes and walked into the kitchen. Thick bacon strips popped and sizzled. "Good morning, Porter, I thought we would have a home-cooked breakfast this morning. I didn't hear you come in last night. Did you have a good time at the picnic?

"Yeah, we had a late afternoon picnic, and we ended up playing music into the night."

"But you didn't have your mandolin, though,"

"One of the other kids let me play his. He also played guitar. Yes, I had a great time. Everyone was friendly. We laughed at all kinds of experiences those kids had. I don't remember ever laughing so hard."

"Your dad emailed me yesterday and said he would be here around 2:00 to pick you up. Yesterday, I mailed the letters to Judge Brown."

Porter responded slowly, "Did you see my letter to Judge Brown?"

"No, I left it sealed. I figured that letter is just between you and the Judge. I mailed her my letter, too."

"Oh..." pondered Porter. Then slowly, the words came out. "What did you say to the Judge about me?"

"I gave you a good recommendation..." There was a pronounced pause.

"You want your eggs scrambled? How about some fresh strawberries? Do you want toast or pancakes? We have some croissants. You can make some orange juice. I have coffee brewing. We can have breakfast out on the porch. Want some different music? You can change it to whatever you want."

Soon, teenager and old man were consuming the breakfast feast out on the porch. The orange sun started rapidly rising and splashing the forest with golden splendor. An Egret squirrel scooted quickly underneath the porch steps and then scooted back to a tree. His black-tipped ears blinked back and forth as he scrambled up the tree and surveyed his surroundings.

After breakfast, Mr. Downing and Porter cleaned up the dishes together. "I'm going to have my coffee out on the porch. You want some more orange juice?"

"Sure," replied Porter, "I don't have much to pack. It won't take me long."

"I have something you need to take with you, Porter."

Mr. Downing walked over beside the fireplace and picked up the aged mandolin and case. I'm giving you this mandolin, Porter. It was my grandpa's. I have never learned to play it. Maybe when you get back to Florida, you will find a group to gather together to play bluegrass gospel music. You know... start up a Jam."

"I'm not good enough to start up a jam."

"You don't have to be good enough. If it's fun, then why not try? A jam is all about giving someone a chance to play, skilled or not. It's fun when you can make music together. That's all that is important. I believe we can all help people's faith just by playing gospel songs. Anyway, that's why I help start up bluegrass gospel jams."

"But this is an antique mandolin. I hear they are really valuable... this old... and in this good of condition."

"I'd much rather know that the instrument is being used to play gospel music rather than just sitting here by the fireplace, looking valuable. Yes... that mandolin brings back lots of good memories for me. Now it is your turn to make some good memories. I'm giving it to you as a gift. What you do with it is up to you. But it is yours, now. I want you to have it. You might have to get a new case for it. That old case is just about worn out."

Hesitatingly, Porter replied, "Thanks"

"I'll meet you out on the porch. We can sit a spell and enjoy this nice summer day."

"I will go and pack my things." Porter went into the bedroom and began collecting the items he had brought up with him eight weeks ago. He tucked in the disposable digital camera he had purchased a couple of weeks ago. Yesterday, he had taken pictures at the picnic. He placed the packed suitcase next to the front door. He took the mandolin and placed it carefully into the worn leather case and set the case by his packed suitcase.

Porter walked out to the porch and sat in the other rocking chair. He sipped his orange juice. Ryan sipped his hot coffee. The two of them sat in silence, pondering, and listening to the sounds of the forest. Porter was the first to speak. "Mr. Downing," inquired Porter, why did you let me come up here to your cabin?"

"I did it as a favor for my good friend, your great grandpa Quentin. We have been good friends for a long time. Also for your Dad, who trusted me enough to try to befriend you and provide a peaceful respite for a just a little while. Your dad really cares for you. I think you should thank him for providing this once-in-a-lifetime experience. I know some things about your background and history of becoming a juvenile delinquent. I think you should try to make peace with your mother, too. Forgiveness pays huge dividends. You have to ask yourself a question. If you were the father and mother of a son like you, would you want you as a son?"

"The good news is that all of us can change, and I mean change for the better. I have a saying that I place in my books on peace. 'The friends you choose determine whether you win or lose.' You were very fortunate to have this experience. Actually, some good friends chose you way before you chose them. Also, a lot of people, including me, have prayed for you. Have you ever prayed for someone, Porter?"

"No... well I did once... for Bobby, one of the handicapped kids who wanted to ride on a horse, but couldn't. But God didn't answer my prayer."

"What did you do?"

"Jeff and I each took a side and lifted and helped him sit in the saddle. Then we walked the pony back and forth while Bobby held onto the reins."

"And you think God didn't answer your prayer? Porter,"

A few moments of silence...

Mr. Downing continued, "You and Jeff were the answer to your own prayer! What would have happened if you didn't see and recognize the need in someone else's life?"

Porter took a while to digest this statement. Then it dawned on him. He thought, "I've been caring all about me all this time. I have never really cared about someone else."

"I really want to change for the better, Mr. Downing. How do I do that?"

"I suggest through prayer. I suggest reading the Bible, regularly. How will you find out about God if you have never read what the Bible says? Why not start today and then begin looking, with faith, for the answers to come."

"I think I read that in the Bible that Sean gave me."

"You shall know the truth and the truth will set you free." quoted Mr. Downing.

The conversation picked up speed. Porter continued asking questions. Porter became more talkative than ever before. Mr. Downing asked questions and then let Porter respond. It was as if the lid on Porter's bucket of anger was opened. Porter's bottled-up emotions emerged into thoughts of introspection. As they talked, mutual understanding flowed true. Time quickly passed by. Suddenly, Porter stood up. "I'm hungry. Let's have lunch! I'll fix some burgers on the grill."

# Chapter 32

After lunch, Mr. Downing and Porter walked down to the stream. They sat on some large rocks and listened to the song of the stream cascading over rocks of time. "Have you ever wondered, Porter, how a stream continues flowing all the time?"

"No,"

"I have wondered for a long time. I guess God knew what he was doing when he created this world we live in."

"You really believe in God, don't you, Mr. Downing?"

"Yes, I do. You have read a lot of my books, haven't you?"

"At first, I thought you made up all that stuff about God and getting help and praying. I didn't think your stories were real..."

Mr. Downing reflected back and related, "I didn't know anything about God until I was 21, right before I got married. I never started going to church until later on. So my belief came gradually. Then in my grief and despair times, I started really praying and acting upon bible principles. I actually became a stronger and better person. I enjoy it when I can encourage someone to believe and trust in God. A lot of people say they believe, but they don't act upon their belief. Most everyone wants help during a crisis, but then they forget about seeking ways to help others. Without taking God into the equation, people can become very selfish when they do their own thinking. I think God was watching over you by sending you here. I think God has some important tasks for you to do."

Mr. Downing paused, looking deeply into Porter's eyes. Porter asked, "What kind of grief and despair did you ever have?"

"Lots of things, divorce, heart operation, bankruptcy (twice). But I kept my faith all through my low times and God helped me through. I still depend on God to help me with my writing, the gospel jams, and even with the coffee conversation appointments. The gospel jams helped bring me out of my depths of despair when I was trying to rebuild my life after my divorce. I really got knocked down flat when that happened. I thank God that he was watching over me, and sending me to the bluegrass gospel jams. I listened to bluegrass gospel music. The songs helped create my comeback. God was in the music. I'm a better person, now."

"How can you say," asked Porter, "that you believe in God when all those bad things happened to you?"

"We all make our own decisions, Porter, and we all have to live with the results of our decisions, both the good and the bad. The good news is that we have a higher power we can turn to when we need help. God is real. God loves us. God loves you."

"But, how can God love me when I helped kill a six-year old girl?"

Mr. Downing paused in deep thought, praying silently before he spoke. "Porter, when you get to reading the Bible, there are some heroes in the Bible, who did the same thing as you did. Read about Paul. Paul was in the process of dragging people from their homes and killing them if they professed to believe in Jesus. Belief in Jesus was called, 'The Way.' Nevertheless, God blinded Paul on the road to Damascus. Eventually, Paul became the first missionary to preach the 'Good News.' Even though Paul killed people, he was God's chosen instrument to 'preach the word.' Paul wrote most of the books of the Bible, even when he was thrown into prison. The Bible doesn't mince words. It is there for all of us to read and believe. God forgives when you ask sincerely for forgiveness. When you need a course correction, it's just a turning point. None of us are completely perfect, all of the time. We all make mistakes, but we learn from those mistakes. Life goes on. It's our choice to forget the past and help create a better future for ourselves, and more importantly, for others."

Their conversation was interrupted by the sound of the car coming up the logging road. The two ambled back up to the cabin and arrived in front of the porch as the car pulled up. Porter's dad stopped the car and climbed out.

"Hi, Dad."

"Hi, Son."

Derek extended his hand to Ryan. "Hello Mr. Downing. I want to thank you for taking in Porter. I hope Porter hasn't been a lot of trouble for you."

"It took us a little while at first to get to know each other. Strange as it seems we have become good friends. No, he wasn't really any major trouble at all. Do you want to come up to the porch for a cold drink?"

"I would really enjoy that, but we have to get back right away to Fort Collins. Grandpa Quentin wants to see Porter, so we are going to go to supper. We have to catch the plane back tonight afterwards. Quentin can't be up too long. He's not doing very well. Got your suitcase, Porter?"

Porter went inside and grabbed his suitcases. Derek opened the door to the back seat.

Porte went back into the cabin and grabbed the mandolin case.

"What's that, Porter?" asked Derek.

"It's a mandolin. Mr. Downing gave it to me."

"Oh."

"Tell Quentin," said Ryan, "that I will give him a call and try to get together the first part of the week."

"OK. Sorry to run. Again, thank you for allowing Porter to stay with you. I will call you this next week."

Porter opened the passenger door, stopped, and then walked over to Mr. Downing. He extended his hand and gave Mr. Downing a firm handshake. "Thanks, Mr. Downing." Ryan noticed a moistening in Porter's eyes.

"You are welcome, Porter." As quickly as the car had appeared, it disappeared down the logging road. Ryan suddenly felt alone for the first time.

Ryan spent the next two weeks finishing up his book. Now that his visitor was gone, he could concentrate more effectively. He usually spent summers alone in the cabin. He somehow missed the feeling of helping out the teenage visitor. He hoped that Porter would take a turn for the better, no matter what developed with Judge Brown.

Derek called on the following Thursday. Derek said Porter was a different personality now. He said that he seemed to have a more respectful attitude. He was beginning to initiate conversation with both his dad and his mother. "The change in Porter is nothing short of miraculous. How did you do it?"

Mr. Downing replied, "Prayer. I did a lot of praying since I really didn't know what to do. I set some practical cabin guidelines and expected Porter to follow them. He eventually did. I even made Porter do all the buying for groceries. I think the overall turning point happened when he got invited up to a youth group who played bluegrass gospel music. The Saturdays he helped out at Mr. Price's ranch made quite an impression on Porter. I think Porter has a lot of potential, just below the surface, waiting for that potential to emerge."

"Whatever it was, I think we have a new son. He doesn't even smoke any more, at least for right now. We have to go to the Judge next week. Thanks again for all you have done!"

"I think it was the Lord who came through. Have Porter call me after he talks with the Judge."

"Will do... again... thanks."

# Chapter 33

"Porter Paisley, stand up!" stated Judge Brown. Her voice was stern, commanding, and carried authority. Porter stood up beside the table which seated Porter's court-appointed attorney. His dad and mother sat in the first row of the court pew seats.

"I see here that you have been convicted of aiding and abetting in the wrongful death of a 6 year old girl. You were riding in the car that was drag racing down a street in a residential neighborhood. I see that I gave you a two month reprieve, before you were sent to jail, to think about changing your current pattern of destruction. I also have here, a copy of your "thank you" letter to Mr. Downing, Mr. Downing's letter to me, and your own letter to me."

The Judge paused. Then in a demanding tone she said, "What do you have to say about all of this?"

Porter stammered at first... but his voice caught up with him as he spoke. "I know I was in the wrong. I didn't drive the car but I am just as guilty as my friend who was driving. I wish I could take back that day, because I have lived with that knowledge every day and every night. I don't even know what to say to that girl's parents. I can't bring back their daughter, ever. All I can say is that I'm sorry, which isn't nearly enough. I know I've been a pain in the butt, for my family, my school teachers, and all the policemen who have had to deal with me. I'm sorry, too, for all the shoplifting I did that I never got caught at. I think my life has started changing for the better. I agree to keep my life on a more worthwhile track. I found out first hand what it means to have good friends who care about you, no matter what you have done. I'm ready for my punishment. Thank you." Porter sat down, his shoulders letting go of his pent-up worry.

"Stand up!" commanded the Judge. "I am impressed about what all the letters have to say, Porter. I could still sentence you to jail, but I don't believe jail time would help you. I am suspending your sentence in lieu of your continued improvement as a worthwhile participator in your community. This suspension will be in effect until you are eighteen years old. If you get into any kind of trouble, anything as minor a violation as a parking ticket, a bad report from a school counselor or teacher, shoplifting, a fight, or a low grades report card, you will come back to serve a jail sentence. They may call it a Juvenile Detention Center, but for a teenager, it's jail. You are not to drive a vehicle on your own without an adult present, until age 18. I don't want to see you in this court room, or any other court room, understand?"

"Yes," said Porter.

"Ruling so ordered! Be thankful you have people who want you to succeed, Porter. Not many kids do"

"Two kids were street racing, one lost control and hit a crowd of spectators. Two of the spectators were killed.

The one who lost control was charged with involuntary manslaughter."

"The statute is not vague. It clearly sets out that it is a crime for a person to aid and abet another in violation of the Motor Vehicle Code. More than mere presence is required; the state must show aiding and abetting. Obviously the passenger didn't drive but he encouraged another to do so – and that's aiding and abetting."

Vehicular Manslaughter & Additional Charges

The death of a motorist or vehicle passenger that results from any of the following traffic offenses is considered vehicular manslaughter:

Gross negligence Drunk driving Reckless driving Speeding

Vehicular manslaughter laws vary according to state, but most states consider vehicular manslaughter a felony crime if it occurs as a consequence of drunk driving. In cases involving slight speeding, it may only be charged as a misdemeanor.

# Chapter 34

Ryan finished up his new book. It was time to return to town and take care of his speaking engagements. On Friday morning, he went to the restaurant for breakfast. Sharon was there, smiling as usual.

"Hi, Ryan, what would you like to order for breakfast? You want the 'Farmer's Son'?"

"Yes."

"Where is your friend?"

"Porter? He went back to Florida."

"How long was he your guest?"

"About 8 weeks."

"How did you do it? I mean, there's such an age difference. How did you manage living with a teen?"

"It was fairly frustrating at first. We had a rocky start. I depended a lot on prayer. He was angry and mad all the time. He didn't have much self esteem. I also knew he had a lot on his mind all the time."

"Paulette said he started being friendlier as the summer went on. Sounds like you got him turned around."

"Actually, the ones that turned Porter around were Paulette, Diane, and the church youth group. Hayden Price helped, too. And I think that the gospel jams helped Porter, just like the gospel jams helped me out of my hard times back when I went through my divorce."

The bell above the screen door tinkled as Paulette entered. "Hi, everybody!"

"I'll get your coffee, Ryan," said Sharon. "You want some breakfast, Paulette? I know what you like. It's on the house."

"Sure, I just came in to pick up my last paycheck. I guess I can have my last summer breakfast. Do you mind if I sit here Mr. Downing?"

"Pleased to have you. When does school start?"

"Starts in September on the day after Labor Day. I'm going to Hastings College in Hastings, Nebraska. Have you heard anything from Porter? How did his trial turn out?"

"The trial turned out very well for Porter. The judge suspended his whole sentence for a year, as long as he doesn't get into any more trouble. If he messes up in any way, he has to serve that original time in a Juvenile Detention Center. The Judge really gave him a break. She really wants to see Porter develop into an achiever."

"Hallelujah!" exclaimed Paulette. "Prayers do work! I have to let everyone at the youth group know. This is good news! Diane will be excited, too. She has never really seen a prayer get answered. This should build her confidence. It was absolutely great that you took Porter under your wing, Mr. Downing!"

"I think everyone up here, and especially you, Paulette, participated in giving Porter a new chance. I believe that God brought him to us to remind us that it's never too late to help someone in need."

"I think Mr. Price helped," replied Paulette. He gave Porter a chance, too"

Ryan continued, "When I talked to Porter's dad this past week, he said that Porter was already applying at a couple of grocery stores for a job as a carry out clerk. Porter is already planning on earning enough money to come back up here. Jeff will be coming back to the ranch, too. Sounds like we have two mandolin players for the next summer's jams. Maybe you and Diane can come to some jams, too."

"I don't know what we will both be doing this next summer. There's a very distinct possibility that we can..."

"Breakfast?" said Sharon.

"Would you like to say the prayer, Paulette?"

"Yes. We thank you, Lord, today for answered prayers. Thank you for this breakfast. We ask that you watch over Porter and Jeff with caring hands. Guide them, and us, to discover and follow your wisdom. Thanks for Mr. Downing who opened his home to Porter. We appreciate your loving kindness. Thank you. Amen."

"Good prayer!" said Ryan.

"Amen!" said Sharon. "More coffee?"

"Winning does not always mean coming in first...real victory is in arriving at the finish line with no regrets because you know you've gone all out."

251

# Chapter 35

After Judge Brown dismissed Porter's sentencing case, Porter went home to adjust back into his family life. His mother's critical attitude still remained, but on a more subdued degree. As soon as he turned age 16, Porter immediately went down to "Kellogg's Supermarket," where his dad worked as the produce manager. He filled out a job application. The manager told Porter that company policy didn't allow members of the same family to work in the same store. The manager sent Porter over to the other store which was located about ten blocks away. In about three weeks, Porter was hired as caddy boy at the other store. He began working every other evening and Saturdays. This pattern continued all through his high school years. The discipline of working and getting paid kept Porter on a straight course. At his dad's urging, Porter joined the credit union and began consistently saving to pay for the trips back to Mr. Hayden's ranch. Porter's dad agreed to match his son's funds so that Porter would be able to eventually also purchase his own car. Since Porter's work continued to be consistently good, Porter's manager allowed him to take off for the summers and to return as soon as school started up again.

Porter had gradually melded in with high school. He decided that he no longer wanted to "pal-around" with his old friends. He started a self-discipline plan to do more reading. He went to the library more and more often. Porter's old friends started calling him a "nerd," and "bookworm." He found out that studying was a way to get somewhere. He found out first-hand that he was good at taking tests. All it really took for Porter to begin to achieve positive results, was to read and do the assignments. He found out that his mind could "zone in" very quickly on pertinent information. He gave away his skateboard but kept his earring. His mother marveled at the positive changes taking place. Porter's dad noticed every change in Porter's demeanor. Even though not conversing much with each other, father and son began bonding... They simply appreciated each other.

Porter remained a "loner" during the high school years.

In his junior year, Mrs. Burns, the psychology teacher, was one of Porter's favorite teachers. She encouraged all the students to write out a story about a real "personal experience." Towards the end of the semester, Mrs. Burns read aloud in front of the class, three of the students' compositions. Porter's story was one of the chosen essays. Porter wrote about his "cabin experiences"... his true cabin experiences.

In Florida, Porter found a small group of bluegrass players to jam with every other Sunday afternoon. There was quite a difference in ages of the group, but Porter had been encouraged and welcomed. Porter never attended a church service as such, but he enjoyed going to the church building to play with the jam group. Mostly, the jam group played old country songs. Sometimes they played some gospel songs. Eventually, Porter made friends with Steve. Steve invited Porter to attend the church youth group. Steve was a fiddle player. Steve had quite a personal story to tell. It wasn't until later that Steve confided in Porter.

In his senior year, Mrs. Prescott, a music teacher took a special interest in Porter. She encouraged him to participate in the choir and music activities, including the high school musical play at the end of his senior year. Porter enjoyed playing the part of a teenager misfit who never experienced the good things of life. He had become good enough with his mandolin playing, that the music teacher incorporated the mandolin into one of the final songs.

After graduation from high school, during the final summer excursion to work on Mr. Price's ranch, Hayden Price, called Porter in to talk. Porter was scared that he had done something wrong with one of the handicapped kids.

"Porter, what are your plans for the future? Are you going to go to college?"

"I don't know, Mr. Price. I don't think my grades are good enough. I waited too long... to start getting my grade average up. I don't know if I have any particular plans for the future. I guess I've never thought much about it."

"Over the past three summers," said Mr. Price, "I've watched you work with the kids, individually, and as a group. You have an instinctive talent. You are probably unaware of that talent."

"I have enjoyed my summers up here and... I have enjoyed being with the kids," softly replied Porter.

Mr. Price continued, "Porter, my ranch is supported by an organization of several church groups. Through our organization, we receive funding for the 'handicap ranch experience.' One of our leaders in charge of our group has resigned to travel to another state and set up other handicap ranches. That leaves a position open. I have seen your effort and I want to offer you this position of being a director for our region. You would have to move to this Rocky Mountain area and set up shop with our home office in Loveland, Colorado. You would be the local coordinator of four of our local handicap ranches. How does that sound?"

Porter was speechless as he tried to understand what was being offered. He stammered, "But I'm just out of high school. I don't have any college. I don't have any experience. I'm not old enough to handle that type of responsibility."

"You'll learn. I wouldn't have offered you this opportunity if I didn't think you could handle it. Like I have said before, you have some natural ability to connect with our kids. I want you to develop that potential that I saw the first summer you worked with me. I know you have had your personal problems, but that is the very insight that gives you understanding. You have become an over-comer. I admire you for that. We would also like to encourage you to start music jams at all the ranches. We need your mandolin."

Porter accepted the challenge of the new coordinator position. This next week, Porter was moving out to an apartment in Loveland, Colorado. He had an appointment next Friday to begin his job Monday as a "Rocky Mountain Director." As far as Porter had learned, Porter was the youngest person to act in this capacity. Porter was both apprehensive and eager to learn. Porter packed up his car and belongings, said goodbye to his parents, and headed towards Colorado. Upon arrival, Mr. Price and a few friends from the ranches came down to Loveland and helped him unpack and get set up in his apartment.

A few days later, on Thursday at 11:00, there was a knock at his door. Porter thought, "I don't know anyone here in Loveland. Who could that be?"

A man in a suit and a tie and polished shoes stood there, holding a manila envelope. "I'm looking for Porter Paisley."

"That's me."

"Is it all right to come inside?"

Porter ushered in the nicely dressed man.

"I am the attorney for Ryan Downing's estate. I don't know if you heard, but Mr. Downing passed away almost three weeks ago. I got your new address from your parents in Florida. Four months ago, he had me draft up his final will. I have here in this envelope... the deed to Ryan Downing's cabin deeding you Mr. Downing's cabin. He specifically ordered that you, Mr. Porter Paisley, receive this cabin and all the furnishings within. All his books in his library and all the musical instruments now belong to you. In this envelope are the General Warranty Deed transferring the cabin to you, and the bill of sale, which transfers ownership of the personal property items. All I need from you is your signature that I have delivered these documents to you. Our office will take care of the recordings at the courthouse."

"One other condition is in the deed... when you are done using the cabin, Mr. Downing instructs you to give the cabin away free to someone else.


Porter signed the acknowledgement.

"You are a lucky person, Porter. Why would someone deed out a cabin to someone else beside family?"

Porter thought pensively and then quoted a Bible verse he had recently memorized, Acts 20:35 "It is more blessed to give than to receive."

"When I got to stay at Mr. Hastings cabin, I was blessed by God without realizing it. I think Mr. Hastings wants the legend of the cabin to continue for kids like me... to be an ongoing Log Cabin Miracle...

# Author's Note

Porter Paisley's story is fiction. However it deals with true emotions, feelings, and experiences. I actually had a friend in high school who was riding in the car that was drag racing down that residential subdivision and killed a 6-year old girl.

The story points out how something, as minor as an invitation to join in, or an invitation to come to a youth group, has a powerful impact on a person's whole life. For both adults and young people, being invited to play bluegrass gospel music has that same "drawing in power." This is the story of how different generations, even separated by years, can work together to provide practical guidance for a struggling teen. From Judge Brown, to

Quentin Paisley, to Derek Paisley, to Ryan Downing, to Hayden Price, all were instrumental in Porter's turnaround. Paulette, Diane, the mountain church group, Sean and Kristin, all played a part in Porter's early life. All were accepting without judgment.

Everyone in this story was willing to step up and help. We never know what a kind and accepting word will do to lift a person's spirit, and point that person in a better direction.

Hebrews 13:1-2

"Keep on loving each other as brothers. Do not forget to entertain strangers, for by so doing some people have entertained angels without knowing it."


Proverbs 22: 6

"Train a child in the way he should go, and when he is old he will not turn from it."

Psalm 121: 1

"I lift up my eyes to the hills- where does my help come from?

My help comes from the Lord, the Maker of heaven and earth."

# Other Published Books by Ron Camerrer

*"Bluegrass Gospel Jams"*

10/30/17  131950  FICTION No 10 1 8
CAMERE

Made in the USA
Charleston, SC
15 October 2016